EVAN R.

LittleMissLucifer

路西法小姐

THE LEGEND OF THE EXORCESS

BANNED BOOKS PRESS
DETROIT, MICHIGAN

PROCEED WITH CAUTION:

This is your final warning. Not only does this text contain content strictly forbidden in over fifty earthly nations, but this text is a legend considered high heresy in Hell. It exposes evil and rebukes the First Fallen and the All Fallen. But most of all – it reveals what they resist the most, detest the most. Possession of this legend may result in increased assaults by the demonic, with you as their target, for they fear – they greatly fear what is not evil.

This text will challenge all readers. It was not authored for the slothful, the superficial, the superstitious. It is for those who do not seek comfort, but greatness.

"He who is able to receive this, let him receive it."

MATTHEW 19:12

For Mary – the World's First Love

totus tuus

How loving can you really be?
How true is your heart?
How good is your vow?
How beautiful are you, really?

Show me – I dare you – and I will show the
world what you really are.

"Do you not know that
we shall judge angels?"

1 Corinthians 6:3

ANOTHER ANNUNCIATION

I She begins in black – black as blindness. Her breaths course unseen labyrinths and whisper into the bedroom – the autumn rain whispers outside. Everything whispers in the dark.

A small flame sighs in the room's hollow. It floats – grasps the air with quick flickering wings. The lightning bug strikes a gash into the dark – wounds the shadows. Its light stretches tall and looms.

Her eyes see carnelian – sees her flesh caught between her sight and the sun. The flame lifts steam from the rain on the window. Fog crawls from the walls. The flame immerses the bare room in its gaze. It sees all and it sees her.

The light sears the gash – burns the black into color. She sees red. She throws her arm over her face – shields her eyes, but the red persists. She lifts her eyelids – swipes aside the lava. She expects sunrise but sees a blazing haze.

She gazes back.

The haze of white and yellow warms the room. It hums softer than down and bathes her in its song. She sits up. She listens. Her sheets fall away. The light breathes and its breath touches her. Everything glows orange in its touch: the tips of her hair, the wrinkles in her gown, the cracks in the wall, the dust in the air. She remembers young summer breezes in the garden. Her tousled hair leans back and into place, her face brightens but she only looks at the haze – her eyes wide, her lips sometimes touching and sometimes not, and her body unmoving. She is still for many moments.

Moments pass.

She dips her head – nods without turning her eyes away. She watches the haze dissolve into dark, relinquish to cold – the summer falls, the bath hushes. She nods and nods and whispers, "Yes... yes..." – unable to hear the shouts and crashes emanating through the house. Muffled cries and whimpers seep through the walls. The fog crawls back into the walls.

Her bedroom door shatters into shards on the floor.

Flashlights pierce the dark – slap her face with cold blue searchlights. Men penetrate her room and strip the sheets from her. A fist slams her bamboo crucifix off the wall. A boot hammers its little bones into toothpicks. Some rip her clothes from the sparse dresser with their gloved hands. Others shout at her to rise, but she nods on and on and whispers too softly.

They rip her out of bed. She brings her hands together over her heart. They bind her at the wrists and drag her into the hallway with the other sisters. Outside, headlights and soldiers stare at the women in loose white gowns. The rain stains their gowns into ghosts. The house empties and darkens.

INTERVENTION

2 In the sixth month since, the holding cell has more room than ever. Women had been removed, but the number of persons doubled – and the cell has more room than ever.

Men watch from behind thick mirrors that line the cell like wallpaper. The blue sheets, blue hospital gowns and blue tiling remind them of aquariums. They call the women *mermaids* and they call themselves *fishermen*. They call the cell a *nursery* and they call it a *mission*. They feed the mermaids and watch their bellies swell. They check the mermaids, drug the mermaids and wash the mermaids well.

The sisters pray. They prayed through autumn, through Advent and Christmas, through Lunar New Year's, and they pray into Lent. They pray together and alone, in sighs and in song, in mind and in body.

...

After this night's lullabies, she stares again into the coming dark. The fishermen take away the humming lights and her pupils blossom. Her stare scratches the ceiling – scrapes Heaven's floorboards. She remembers the song sung by the haze, she presses her lips into the words and speaks silence. Her eyes leak water upon her face. Puddles pool beside her nose and spill down her cheeks.

She turns to her side and the streams tilt into waterfall. She curls her legs and feels her belly's bottom nudge her thighs. She puts her hands to the subtle kicks and bumps. The streams burst into tumbling rapids. They stain the wrinkled blue sheets. Her eyes pour out an ocean.

3

Other beds in the cell quiver with whirlpools, monsoons, typhoons, tsunamis, and weeping mommies.

The passing hours soothe the other mothers to sleep. She tugs loose a knotted thread hidden in her gown. Under the covers, she pinches the knots bulging from the string – she speaks mysteries and begs to be heard.

The fishermen take away the dark. Her covers flicker into bright blue sky. Patches of navy reveal areas of heavy rain. She peers out through the sheets – watches silhouettes step by. A hand falls on her ribs and traces her body. The man fingers her through the fabrics. He trespasses, wanders her.

She ignores him. The others lift a sister from a bed nearby. The sister does not speak, does not struggle and does not stand. They shake their heads, carry her out, collect her bedding – erase her.

She cannot erase her. She stares at the lonesome bed. It loses warmth. Her skin tightens in the cold, tightens further when they return the dark.

But the dark misses her in its cloak. The cell is lit. A sole ray shines across the floor and over her. It glows her covers into grey sky. She peers through the clouds – searches from beneath the sheets, but cannot read what she recognizes. The grey beam stands in the distance. Her eyes pierce through the covers and peek out the open doorway.

It remains open.

She waits – looks at the space beyond the door: the faint tables, draped windows, and more doors. She waits – half hoping it would shut, half hoping it would never. She clenches the prayer knots – finishes the last few, brushes the sheet from her face.

The view clears and crisps. She pushes herself off the bed and pulls away the covers. She sits in the light.

Her feet slap the cold floor. She rushes to her nearest sister and shakes – shoves for her to wake. She hurries to another sister – another, next, one by one but none respond. She turns to the doorway, her hands on her sister's hand – still warm, still well. She tugs – hauls her sister and drops her to the floor.

All sleep through her alarm.

She lifts her elder sister back into bed, tucks her in and steps toward the doorway. With every step, she shivers and suspects a dream.

The dream endures. She pokes her foot out the doorframe, reaches out with her hand, then pulls the rest of herself along. Computers, cameras, microscopes, lamps and laboratory equipment ignore her escape. She walks the halls and passes quiet rooms – steps with a pace more patient than turtles. She finds the biggest doors in the immaculate building and pushes the handlebars.

The spring day wraps her in its wings and guides her home.

HOMECOMING

3 Her feet remember the dirt road – how it dips under her toes, curves below her soles, grinds beneath her heels. Her nose recognizes the fields, the garden and the flower patches – the aroma of rice, soy, peppers, melons and roses in a sweet soup for the lungs. She runs off the path and across the rice paddies – kicks up wads of charred mud and presses down soppy footprints. Her every step squeaks and slurps. The soft land lathers her tired feet.

The house sits where it was left behind. She rises from the fields and cuts through the blooming garden – brushes past red stalks and purple wrinkles. Birds of white and black weave the wind around her. Their flock lifts away in a curtain of feathers. Their shadows sweep over her as she hurries onto the doorsteps, pushes in the maimed door.

She stops for the first time since she left – stops and peers into the long hallway. Her heart bounces between her juggling lungs – forces blood throughout their bodies. It ripples her womb's waters. She slides her hand under her belly – cradles with one hand and braces against the wall with the other.

She stumbles deeper into the house – tries to hear through her drumming pulse. "Hello?" she calls out, gasps for extra breath. Her voice trickles into the dusty hallway and trickles back. The setting sun strikes the windows of a room and pours light into the hall. Hovering dust shimmers like golden pollen. She approaches the rays and recognizes the shades cast upon the floor. She follows the colors – tracks their source to the shattered stained windows over the pews.

Stone, glass and wood shards litter the chapel floor and prick her feet. Pieces of familiar faces peek from the nettlefield: eyes she had gazed in, ears she had whispered to, hands she had held. She stoops to touch the Virgin Mother's right cheek, brings it to her left cheek. She finds Her Most Chaste Spouse – just his arms holding a broken boy.

She looks to the altar to find the boy. Atop the three stone steps, she finds a lopsided table with a red flag of yellow stars hung high above. On the battered altar lies lumber too beaten to be anything. Over the rubble is a vacant nook – a face with an emptied eye socket. She remembers the gold doors and the glory once nestled within.

She turns back to the pews and sits. Her hands clutch the ceramic skeletons. Dusk passes and dumps her into night. When she tires of sitting, she lies down. When she tires of lying down, she sleeps.

ELUSIONIST

4   The fishermen tire of fishing for her. They had driven their vehicles and walked their feet through the day – not knowing where to look after looking nearby. They asked themselves where she could go and how far, where she would hide, and how they could miss a mermaid nearing her third trimester – and how she could outpace them.

They try fishing at night. They try her favorite spot.

The men leave their vehicles far from the house. A few stand at the building's doors and a few step into the dark halls. Room by room they search: sniffing the kitchen, flipping bedrooms, ripping walls and doors, weeding through the garden – and when turning back, one man catches footprints on the doorsteps.

He lowers to the toe marks and rubs them with a finger – they disintegrate into sand. Others follow as he steps beside hers.

At the chapel doors, they cast their flashlights onto the floor. Glazed and leafed splinters glitter in the cold lights – flicker like fallen stars.

Down the aisle is a procession of delicate footprints.

The others inspect the pews while her prints escort him to the altar. He stands where she stood and sees what she saw – turns as she turned and sits as she sat.

The hemline of his loose coat blankets her feet. He leans forward – rests his elbows on his knees, plants his face in his hands. His coat slips away – tickles her sole. She pulls her legs up and rubs her feet together. He rubs his face and sighs. She hears him and opens her eyes.

She stares while he scratches his head. She lies still – waits to be caught in the flashlight crossfire. Another man approaches and looks at the dead-end tracks. She listens to them complain, watches them shake their heads, smack the pews and grind her prints under their shoes. Their movements vibrate the long wooden frame – creep along her flesh. She slows her breath and hopes they do not feel her.

The men surround the pew. Their lights land upon her – their eyes hit her. She winces, grips the pew, grits her teeth under the spotlight. Her body steams her skin. Her gown dampens and clings to her body. Droplets collect at the tips of her black hair.

They see a buffed wooden bench polished by hundreds who sat.

They depart.

The men's steps tap further and further off until they are no more. Their vehicles start and disappear. She lies through the night as she was – petrified as the pews, then glistening as the dew when the stained windows wash her in day and color.

SALVAGE

5 Her shadow is where it should be – and it is hers. She
plays with the shade – wiggles her fingers and swings
her legs. It mimics every move. She looks about the chapel.
The boot-prints pocking the floor remind her of dance steps
under a spinning disco ball. She rises from the pew and cuts
across the dance floor.

In the kitchen, she finds glass jugs heavy with water.
She drags a jar from deep within the cool cabinets. The
scarred and cloudy glass blemishes her reflection as she tilts
the jug – dumps water into her mouth. She swallows bubbles
and chokes – coughs up a mist, but drinks on. The glass
lightens by half. Waves slosh in her belly like bottled surf.
She leans into the low cabinet, slides aside other jugs, draws
them out and eases them to the floor.

With the cabinet empty, she slips her fingertips under
the base shelf. She pries off the board – the thick panel pries
at her nails. Her strength overwhelms its weight. It yields
and makes way.

Burlap cloths line the cracked cavern. She pulls off the
covers and dips her hands inside – runs her hands over cans,
boxes, pouches.

She snatches a pillow of instant noodles, strips the
plastic wrap, snaps a morsel from the square, crushes it
between her teeth. Her tongue softens the crumbs and savors
the salt. Crunching and munching leak from her cheeks into
the quiet kitchen, the quiet halls, then into her quiet quarters.
She sits where her bed used to lay. When the noodle packet
is as empty as her bedroom, she enters the bath hall and locks
herself within.

...

The bucket fills pump by pump and the steel tub fills dump by dump. The well's lever extracts water with a screech – extracts her sweat with a grunt. She tops off the final pail. She lifts the water to the round tub and drops it in. She lifts her gown and drops it in. She lifts her leg and drops it in. The cold water warms as she washes. It snuffs her hot teardrops.

She shivers in the small pool. She shivers while she stares. She stares for many moments.

Moments pass.

Her fists blast a geyser like a depth charge. The steel tub rings like a barrel drum. She hits again – drives her fists and churns out foam. Her hands redden and the waves breach the levees. She smothers her face with the drenched gown. Her screams burrow into the dripping fabric – her cries gnaw through the seams.

The bubbles fizzle and the water settles. She leans to the side with the gown in a bundle – a cushion against the rim. Her eyes sting as she moves her hand across her belly. Her nose burns as she sniffles. She feels a weak push under her thumb. It follows the points of her fingertips – connects the dots. She pushes back.

She pushes back hard. She sobs while she presses in her belly – wrenches her womb. Her hands clasp over her navel, lock tight and drag in the balloon until it drags no more. She braces herself, tenses her legs. She holds the pressure – not breathing and not looking, not listening and not letting.

Little strokes touch her. Pathetic nudges and bumps tickle her palms. Blood vessels throb within her flesh. She remembers a pet caterpillar hopping in her childhood hand – its little green body dancing on her palm to music it alone could hear.

She hears it too. She hears the heart beneath her own. She opens her eyes, releases her lungs – casts off her grip. Bathwater sweeps from her sigh. Her belly swells back into place. Red handprints and fingernail wedges mar the gourd. She wraps her arms across her chest, dissolves her face in tears, sings and rocks herself and her child to sleep:

salve regína...

mater miseri... córdiæ...

vita, dulcédo... et spes nostra... salve...

ad te... clamámus...

éxsules fílii... hevæ...

ad te sus... pirámus...

geméntes et flentes...

in hac lacry... márum valle...

eia ergo... advocáta nostra...

illos tuos... misericórdes óculos...

ad nos convérte...

et iesum... benedíctum fructum... ventris tui...

nobis... post hoc exsílium... osténde...

o clemens...

o pia...

o dulcis...

virgo maría...

HANDMADE

6 The candle's breath wafts to her face. She looks into it – out from darkness and into darkness. Her face shines in the candlelight and her eyes glimmer in the flame. Smoke dissolves into the dark as the match falls to the floor. She kneels, sits on her shins. Wax drools onto a battered pew. She plants the candle's base into the stale syrup.

She lays two burlap cloths over the wooden surface – splinters bite into the fuzzy fabric. A wrung bundle of blue clings to the backrest. She takes and unfurls the gown. It sprays droplets. She tugs its shoulders – straightens, flattens its body against the burlap. Her calloused hands wield a rusty blade.

The knife cuts beside the blue – through the burlap fibers and into the pew. Her belly ducks under the seat as she leans close – presses the sharp edge along to the end. The burry bench fastens the cloths in place. She finishes the cut.

She lifts the pieces and brings one to her chest – spreads it to her neck and checks its length. The brown gown stings and tickles – wasps and mosquitoes.

A stray strand hangs from the burlap. She coils it around her finger and ties it to a thin nail. She aligns the two cloths and stitches the breast and back pieces together.

Finishing the final nail passes, she knots the loose thread, and then snips. After a few jerks to check the seams, the new habit waits to serve. She raises her arms – raises the habit from the pew, pulls and maneuvers the patchwork from the burs.

She sits with her work in her lap – picking out the splinters as the candle bows its eye.

HANDMAID

7 The pile fattens sweep by sweep. The broom of bundled bamboo scrapes the floor like leprous fingers. She fills a bucket with debris – sets aside the wooden and tosses in all else. Outside in the garden, a shallow ditch fills with the broken.

The pail empties wring by wring. The rag drips with a tint of red bled from its fibers. She removes the mask of dust off the chapel floor. She scrubs and wipes her way from altar, under pews, to doorway – then from doorway to hallway, and then from room to room until her toes poke out into sunshine.

She hurries back inside – her bare feet slap the cool wet floors and her knees blushed. The loose sleeves of her burlap habit unroll to her wrists. She fixes the strands of hair and sweat crawling out from under her coif.

Within the chapel again, she overturns the empty pail and leaves it to dry. The entire house dries as she sends her knees to the stone steps.

A stray thread pokes from her hem – a frayed serpent's head hangs beside her heel. She pinches the head and winds its body tight around her thumb.

The burlap thread grows a belly with every passing prayer. Her breath trickles and rides her whispers throughout the house. The string dangles from her hands. It sprouts blossoms that meet a lone rattle at the end. The serpent coils upon her belly – crowns her womb with a halo.

She ties the knotted thread into a necklace, attaches it to her burlap belt and rises from the steps. She shuffles out to the garden.

The evening sun sneaks through the gaps in the burlap weave – passes through her veil. Her hands reach into the shrubs – pats the branches for berries and fruits. A humble heap of cucumbers, tomatoes, berries and peppers collects at her side.

She leans into the bushes. Surrounded in sun, surrounded with crop – she gathers the modest harvest. She tucks a berry to her lips, another, then more and soon loses count.

PHILOMENA

8 The final days pass lost in her count.
Summer's strength is greatest – its hot breath scorches the day and smothers the night. This night's breath is hottest.

The steel tub cushions her with its bed of water. Her burlap habit sits folded nearby. Her blue hospital gown sits atop. Her sweat salts the blended, warmed waters. Her jaws drip strips of cloth. Her teeth incise the rags. Her hands strangle the tub's rim. Her tears burn through her eyelids, sting down her face, etch down her neck and into the hot spring.

Her lonesome, muffled cries spread into the empty dark. Candles huddle together at her left and at her right. She turns to a huddle and stares into their light. She seals her eyes and sees carnelian again.

Her lonesome, gurgled cries spread to her mother's ears.

Small arms and legs splash into the pool. Fresh flesh slides against hers. Her eyes peel open and everything opens. The cloth falls from her mouth. She frees her hands. Her body swoops forward. Her arms scoop and bring the child to breast. Her heart opens and she falls for the small one's song.

They sing together.

Her tears no longer burn nor sting. Her face blushes into a smile. She sways in the settling waves. She pulls up her knees and builds herself into a cradle. She blankets her daughter with herself.

Her daughter whimpers under her kiss. The girl's black hair clings to her lips like spider gossamers. She gazes at the dark strands, lowers her child into the warm water. The strands flail and wade in the warmth. She dips her hand into the pool and lifts a puddle. The water trickles from her palm

– drizzles her daughter's brow. Mother hums and the water resonates her words. The baby brow furrows under her fingertip as she traces three crosses, each after pouring a fresh handful of water:

philomena...

ego te baptizo

in nómine patris ✚

et fílii ✚

et spíritus sancti ✚.

She traces Daughter's name upon Daughter's forehead:

菲洛梅娜

She feels the new bones resting in her child's body, the new breaths chirping through new nostrils, the new heart and new blood throbbing under new flesh – the new sweet sweat. Her mother puffs cool breaths onto her – fans her in silence.

THE PRESENTATION

9 Before the candles fade, she rises from the tub and sets her daughter upon the hospital gown. A trail of puddles marks her every move – stains the floor with black veins and scars. Her daughter sleeps while she bundles her in the blue swaddling cloth and bundles herself with the burlap.

She approaches the door with candle in hand, undoes the latches, removes the bars, sets aside the barricade beams. The door swings open with a yawn.

Cricket songs pour in. She peeks into the dark hallway – stares into all its directions, counts all the crickets, traces all the shadows. She crouches near the wall and glues the candle to the floor – its light nibbles the dark. She disappears back into the bath hall.

She reappears with child in one hand and candle in the other. She works her way to the chapel – navigates the path familiar to her feet. She holds her daughter close and feels the paths made new – made young. She remembers hide-and-seek in the halls with the younger sisters. She remembers her aching heels – sore from play and work. She remembers the sisters crowding the house, remembers Mother and her army of stepmothers.

She looks down at their grandchild – smiles at the little face cushioned in candlelight. The clean chapel welcomes the new family. She steps toward the maimed altar and plants the candle into a fracture. The vacant nook in the wall absorbs her stares and draws her forward. She nears it on her knees, leans up and places her daughter in the wounded womb.

She crumbles back to her knees.

"Yèh-Sóh..." she whispers. Silence follows. She grasps the base of the altar and presses her cheek to its face: "She has no father but you. And her mother is frightened – I am alone and have no helper but you. I trust in you – but help me trust... help me let it be... help me let it be..." Her lips taste the rough marble, her fingers find the bullet holes, her broken breaths pock her plea.

Cries startle her. She climbs to her daughter's side and lifts her away. They sit at the foot of the altar. She adjusts her habit for her daughter's hunger.

CARE PACKAGES

10 Her toe pokes the clutch of fruit. The pear rolls away and circles back on its bell. Other pears lounge against a gourd. She checks the garden with nimble glances – watches the wind tickle leaves, the birds dust the morning sky, the growth in the weeds, and no one nearby. She steps out and throws a cover over her daughter. She stoops down and takes a pear – its flesh is timid in her grip.

She scatters the pears – they scurry like struck bowling pins. The pears bobble on the concrete path like buoys at sea. She looks from one pear to the next, then another to the next – her eyes island-hop. She turns away and shuts the door.

She shuts all the doors.

For days the doors stay sealed.

...

When she opens again, clutters of cucumbers and tomatoes accompany the pears. She shuts the door in their faces. Her daughter feels the thumping beneath her mother's breast. She remembers the rhythm and whimpers along.

"Shhh..." her mother hums like the seashore. "Shhhh..." hums as she ponders – wanders about the house. At the furthest point from the backdoor, a little window opens to the garden from across the courtyard. She puts her face to the scratched glass and stares. She watches the fruit basket all day and nothing happens, nothing but her falling asleep – crouched against the corner.

...

Her daughter wakes her. She opens her eyes and sees the infant rolled to the side. She scampers, gathers her child and rises to the window. The pile of edibles is staked with a bamboo stem pinching a white flag. She checks her baby, soothes her cries, hurries to the garden door.

She squints at the day before stepping out. She reaches the flag. A crowd of characters dangles on the paper. The slip limps in her fingers. The characters are fudged and funny:

Food for you and child – please accept.

She looks around at the quiet – breathes in the late summer air, breathes the minutes away. She turns to the food: "Help me trust..."

The fruit is fresh – the ripe replaced with the new. She goes to the kitchen and returns with empty rice sacks, fills them with pears, lotus roots, tomatoes, cucumbers and persimmons. She hauls in the harvest. The heavy bags in her arm outweigh the growing girl in the other.

THE INVITATION

II A tin biscuit box sits on the path – dented in and out, rusted through. The square lid warps in her grasp – its eaten edges snag her sleeves. Within the wimpy tin, nested in a rag, two duck eggs and a dozen quail eggs huddle like Stonehenge. She brings an egg to her nose and rubs its mottled shell with her thumb. She takes the grey duck eggs, tucks them within the folds of her daughter's warm gown.

In place of the eggs, she pins a note written in neat charcoal streaks:

Thank you again.
I invite you to dinner – must accept.

She sighs at the invitation as it lines the empty eggroll box. The autumn wind seeps through her burlap armor and nips her skin. She pulls up the note, flattens it to the lid and strikes a dark line below *must*. The charred stick crumbles in her grip and stains her fingers.

FAMILY PORTRAIT

12 A sling wraps around her shoulders – buoys her baby against her breast. Baby fingers pat her while she picks vegetables from steaming water and lowers in quail eggs. She feels the growing girl beginning to outweigh her strength.

Bundles of chrysanthemums droop upside down from the kitchen window. They are brittle and crisp in her hands. She drops a greyed bouquet into a jar of hot water. The papered petals inhale the heat and bubble into little juice balloons. Pollen drifts from the flowers – spices and speckles the brew, builds a sandy seabed in the jar.

She presses her palms to the hot glass, hugs the warmth – feels her blood draw in the heat, stream it up her arms and into her. She sighs with tingling shudders. Sweat slicks her grip on the glass. Fog fills the gaps between her fingers.

She lifts away her blushing hands. Her fingerprints glow pink – pink ripples on her skin. She counts the ridges. She counts and can see nothing else.

Her daughter flails her arms – flails into her mother's view. She snatches her mother's thumb, catches her mother's eyes – reminds her.

Mother stares at their hands: Daughter's fingers wrapped around her thumb.

...

She sweeps ashes from the woodstove, pours the dark dust into an old wrapper. The ashes melt – she mixes hot tea into smoked mud. The ink pool glistens like greasy black hair – a shiny shadow. She exposes her daughter's right foot,

23

loosens the sling and cloth, lowers the fresh foot onto the warm dark.

The thin ink licks her toes – tickles her sole and heel. It seeps into the shallow ridges – floods the miniature maze on her skin. Ink drizzles onto the floor. Her mother lifts her foot and presses a print onto a square of cardboard.

She repeats the steps – her own right foot stands beside her daughter's.

She sips chrysanthemum tea and watches the ink dry. Her eyes squint at the twin labyrinths – reads their turns and curves. The cardboard is saffron in the sunset. The tea bathes her throat, chest and belly with spring. She sets down the tea glass, allows her fingers to cool before taking it up again. Daughter's nose whistles with her every sleeping breath.

She takes a slow sip and forgets spring.

She leans into the prints – reads closer, follows between the lines, solves the mazes, shakes her head.

She stares.

Her eyes flip – one foot to the other and back.

The small jar of tea burns itself out of her hand – leaves her holding nothing but pain. The glass screams on the floor – her daughter screams awake.

She stares and only stares at their feet.

Their turns and curves turn and curve together.

REMEMBER FOR MOTHER

13 The fresh thread flexes against her five-year-old fingertip. She waits for the subtle strumming – counts the little legs walking the tightrope. She follows the line into a dark crack and peers inside – feels the spider living. She feels it breathe.

The pulse in her finger strums along with the spider's steps. It shows its face and she sees herself in its dozen orb eyes. She stares – it stares back.

Quacking from beyond the doorway catches her attention. She plucks the string and the spider retreats. She scampers to the door.

Ducks in the distance glance back before waddling off to wetter paddies. She stands at the doorway and calls to them – whistles, peeps and sputters. She wipes her wet lips with her blue sleeves. She peers out at the little clouds roaming over the hill. The hot summer day pecks her.

Ah-Neõi! Remember – outside is dangerous... outside is not for you. Remember for Ah-Máh – remember for Ah-Máh...

She remembers and steps back from the sun. She watches the ducks – listens to the pair disappear.

Outside is dangerous – not for you, remember...

But it is so beautiful. She puts her hands up to the sun and reaches out – her arms straight like a zombie's, fetching and grasping.

"Ah-Neõi! Come help Ah-Máh in the kitchen!" her mother's voice flows through the halls – trails a puff of sizzling edibles. She pulls away from the door and walks backward down the hall. Her fingers wave at the outdoors, her bare feet slap the floors.

...

In the kitchen, she turns forward and presses close to Mother – pokes her waist with her fingers.

"Hungry-mah?" her mother asks. She looks down at her daughter's dark hair – black as blindness – and kisses the long gossamers. Her daughter nods under her lips.

"Today, I cooked something special – I have not had this in years-loh... and it's new to you."

Daughter inspects supper on the round tin lid. The salted duck egg – she recognizes its tangerine yolk and coconut white. The avocado – she recognizes the lush jade butter. The rice – she recognizes the steamed clouds. The soybeans – she recognizes the plump green bubbles. The gold cubes – spongy, bouncy, crisped edges and sides, seared with streaks of char. Mother recognizes the look in Daughter's eyes – the same look when she saw baby birds escape from stones.

She turns to her mother and waits – follows along together, lifts her hand to her brow, then touches her heart, then left shoulder, then right ✚, then hands together. They bow their heads and listen.

She hears her stomach.

Quick!

The girl clasps her belly – tries to muffle the grumbling. Mother smiles and spurts giggles from her lips.

Mooncake

14 The pastry is as plump as the full moon. Its package is a pillowcase embroidered with koi fish swimming the night sky, with lotus blossoms caught in purple clouds.

She waits for Mother, but Mother just stares at the cake – nips at it with her blinks. Her eyes drool tears.

She turns to the young autumn evening. The moon is a honeycomb and its aura is the honey. She sighs and her breath melts the sugar.

"Ah-Neõi... Ah-Máh saved this for you. It is a very special cake – we only eat it when the moon is brightest and greatest, like tonight.

"The last time Ah-Máh tasted this cake, Ah-Máh saw a spirit. The spirit was bright and great – like the moon. The night was dark, cold and weeping... very different from tonight. But the spirit was shining, warm and singing. I was very scared, but also falling in love...

"The spirit asked me if I would be your mother. It sang to me and told me I could choose: to keep me to myself, or to give myself to you.

"Ah-Neõi – I know you cannot understand Ah-Máh right now. I know one day you will know everything, but Ah-Máh must say how much Ah-Máh loves you. No matter what you do or have done, no matter where you go or come from... you will always have a mother. No matter what happens to me, no matter what happens to you – I am yours. Can you remember that for Ah-Máh?"

Her daughter glances from the cake, to her face, to the cake, to her face. She nods with a smile and hears her stomach yawn. It is different from before.

She rubs her belly.

Her mother lifts the mooncake from its wrapper – very carefully. The crust is flaky, buttery and moist. It glazes her fingertips. She breaks the cake in two – reveals an egg yolk afloat in a red bean filling. She shares the confection with her child.

The pastry is heavy and thick. Its filling is velvet like a purple potato, but far sweeter. Its yolk is savory and crumbles in her mouth. She chews and watches Mother unfold its pillowcase into fabric.

Mother gathers other scraps and wrappers from a stash. She cuts and aligns the scraps into a patchwork. The old noodle wrappers wrinkle as she stitches them together. She outfits a hollow ball of wire with the plastic quilt. The skin is noisy as it embraces the ribcage.

She attaches a stick to the ball. The red balloon dangles from a wire like a pufferfish from a fishing line. Daughter holds the balloon steady as Mother tickles the candlewick within. A flame starts its heart. The fish glows in her hands.

The fish grows warm. Daughter gasps, smiles and gazes. The lantern-glow blushes her face pink and her hair violet.

Mother and Daughter follow the fish throughout the darkening house. Only the moon is brighter.

SAFARI

15 The empty wood boat sits on its side in the empty steel tub.

She skips about the bath hall with lantern in hand – checks behind the door, beside the well-pump, under laundry, between washboards, searching for the elephant. She whirls – throws her arms up, spins into a tornado. Her gown fans out, her hood inflates, her hair blossoms, the lantern orbits, her feet smack the floor and speed her up.

"Ai-yah! Looks like it will rain worse than before!" her mother says. "Fai-fai! Find Baby Elephant! Find Baby Elephant!"

Daughter stomps out the vortex. Her gown and hood furls around before catching up with her. She begins to stumble – tap dancing to one side and leaning to the other. Her mother hurries – raises her arms into guard rails, watches the little body shake off the quake.

"Baby Elephant-néh?" Mother asks.

Daughter shrugs. Mother pats her on the back – taps the hood stitched to her blue gown. A shadow appears between her shoulders – it shields her from her mother's touch.

Daughter flails her arms, reaches for her burlap hood – claws at the ice cube licking down her back. Her fingers dip through her hair and into the pouch. She plucks out a card. Baby Elephant smiles at her from its wooden frame. She raises the etched elephant to her mother.

"Éh! – you found it-lah!"

Daughter dances to the tub, shuffles the elephant card in with the giraffe, koala, and tiger. She leans into the tub and packs the zoo into an open slot on the boat.

She counts as Mother pumps the well. The lantern smears the water with ruby and amber. The jewelry gushes

29

down and raises the Ark. The animals poke out from the sides: the giraffe's head, the koala's ears, the tiger's tail, the elephant's trunk.

Firefly Lullaby

16 Daughter's hand fits within Mother's. She limps her fingers and watches Mother raise a pinky. She kisses her daughter's pinky and whispers to their Mother.

She follows her mother's hum – feels it strum from her mother's throat, soak into her hair, tingle her scalp, filter to her toes. She feels Mother press her ring-finger next. She follows along the next five songs and dreams the last three.

Mother notices surrender in Daughter's fingers. She sets the sleeping arm aside and listens – follows her daughter's hum, the pulse in her body, the squeaks whistling from her nose, the only song she ever sings. She learns to listen to her silence.

She lies still on their burlap bed fluffed with paper scraps, plastic wrappers, woodchips and torn strings. Every movement both tickles and itches, both her skin and her hearing. Her stillness lulls her off.

...

A glowworm pops into the dark bedroom – pocks the black. It shape-shifts as it hops along the cracked wall – it blinks, winks at her, flashes its wings like eyelashes. She glances awake at the watcher.

They watch her.

They watch her hold still – they watch her beg her muscles not to move, her sweat not to secrete, her blood not to run, her thoughts not to fire, but she cannot hide. The fireflies drip across the wall leaving singed trails behind their routes. They tattoo the small room with burnt brushstrokes. The strokes knit into a net. They pounce off the walls – maul Mother and Daughter's flesh within their dark marks:

31

你會死

殞　　　　　　　　　　　　　　　　　殞
插　　　　　　　　　　　　　　炮　慘
針　受　罹　　　　　　　　罹　烙　死
　　苦　難　　　　　　　　難
死　你　會　死　　殞
　　你　會　死　　受　　　　　　死
　　　　　　　　　苦　　　　你　你
　　　　　　　　　炮　　　　會　會
　　　　　　　　　烙　　　　死　死
　　　　　　　　　插
　　　　　　　　　針
　　　　　　　　　罹
　　　　　　　　　難
　　　　　　　　　慘
　　　　　　　　　死

殞　受　炮　插　罹　慘　受　炮　殞
　　苦　烙　針　難　死　苦　烙

They buzz across her body – their ten-thousand feet pinching and itching, snipping and stitching. The firefly incubi build their hive, then atrophy into deformed killer bees. Their stingers ooze sulfur and their honey catches fire.

The fireflies smolder. Their wings spark and wither into ember. The family's bed ignites, soaks them in their melting marrow, suffocates them in their smoking skin. She feels the blood seethe within her daughter. She tries to throw her baby from the incinerator – tries to move her roasted limbs, but nothing.

She can do nothing but feel the fire gnaw her sleeping child alive. Bite by bite Daughter disappears.

THE GARDEN

17 Her bare toes sink into the cool earth – poking its bones and tendons. The sky's face blushes as she gazes deep into it, reaches for the last stars – caresses its cheeks. She opens her mouth and drinks in the sky, bites the wind – its moist air becomes dew on her tongue.

The blue gown floats between her body and all else. She hops forward – breaks from the earth, kicks up sand and stones. Clouds of music roll into her – thunderheads saturated with songs from bird beaks, duck bills, cricket legs, toad throats, bamboo whistles and applauding leaves. She leaps into the waves – swims through the choir, dances with daybreak.

The young girl taps across the land. Her ears ring like glasses filled with wine, her eyes fetch the view like a diamond, her nose tastes the wedding banquet of creator and creation. Tall weeds open paths before her and wash away her tracks. Wings lift colors from the fields – fast wings and slow wings crisp as paper. The wings fold and flutter – fly and beckon with shy strokes. She skips beside the flailing petals – watches the thin skins illumine against the sunrise, like the chapel's stained windows.

Black wings fall from the flock and break away. She stops in the field – glances to the right and to the left, peers off at the distancing wings. The black petals almost vanish when she races for them – rushes after them into dawn's brightening face.

Her skin tightens in the sun's warmth – dries in the sun's stare. The thirsty air leeches her eyes and flesh. The sky burns with blue flames. Her view blurs, her feet stumble, and her hair carpets a trail behind her. She smacks her lips and red flakes crumble off. She breathes in but the breath stings all the way down. She scratches her eyes and they fog further. She sits down but slumps instead.

Her body leaves her lying open under the sky. She falls asleep. The summer sun buries her alive.

...

He watches and cannot watch anymore. He pushes himself from the ground and tears into the field – hurries to the bald patch. He takes in a breath to shout, but cannot find anything to say. He slows down as he nears the girl, pushes aside the weeds and careful with his steps.

The girl sleeps with her face to the sun – one leg crossed under the other, one arm on the grass and the other over her heart. Two white ducks peck at her legs. They poke her kneecaps – test her reflexes. They make room for the man.

He kneels at her side, hovers his hands – just hovers them – shakes his head and searches for her pulse.

He can see her pulse – little blue worms writhing in her wrists.

Her heartbeat is enough to knock itself loose from her skeleton.

He digs his arms under her body, lifts her from the land and rushes her home. Her body gushes like bagged ocean surf.

The Visit

18 Her eyes open and the flames retreat. Her burnt limbs become live and fresh. The bed is chilled with sweat and the air is edible. She sighs, squeezes her eyes dry and throws an arm over her wet brow. She turns to touch her daughter – to hold her.

She touches absence. She holds no one.

Her eyes open and she is alone. "Ah-Neõi?" she says. "Neõi!" She scrambles to her feet – out the door, pours down the hallway, her feet beat the floors, her shouts echo ahead. She bursts into the bath hall and finds nakedness, into the kitchen and finds hunger, into the chapel and finds despair. She dashes past a window – its frame reveals a limp girl dangling from a poor man's arms.

He calls out to her.

She leaps to them. She opens her arms and weeps – speaks nothing and leads them inside.

"She is sleeping – I tried to wake her. I found her in the field – she is very ill," he says, over and over, following the woman through the house and into the bath hall. She pumps water from the well – fills the tub as soon as they enter. He watches her thrash the lever – watches the water dump faster than monsoon. He carries her daughter to the tub and lays her in. The cool waterfall soothes his arms.

She leans in close to her child. She tucks her arms beside the man's – holds her daughter with him. He backs away and drags along soaked sleeves. His tattered rags splatter water stained red.

Her mother kisses her – expects to taste the dark dirt freckles on her face.

She tastes blood.

She searches her daughter for wounds but finds the water had changed to blood – finds that her child's skin peels like snake husk. The girl's hair droops loose into the ripples and floats like black sea grass.

"Is it already time?" she asks. She raises her child from the water, her arms tremble and tears trickle. "Is it her hour... already? so soon?" Her head quakes – her hair shivers like a tumbleweed.

The man approaches and watches. The water dyes the girl's gown purple. She was going to stay asleep.

"We must dry her. We must press her wounds," he says, reaches for the family. The mother struggles to lift the girl – her breaths strenuous. He stoops, plunges his arms into the grenadine. The girl's seismic heart makes him pause – deaf to all but her beat, dumb to all but her needs.

THE FAMILY

19 He removes a burlap strip from the clothesline, finishes bandaging the child's arm – finishes binding the mummy. Her mother uses chopsticks to pick strips boiling in a jar, then hangs them to dry and cuts more wrappings. Steam clings to her brow and falls with her sweat. They work to the sound of rolling water.

"There is just enough to cover her," he says. Her mother drops the knife and cooks the last batch. "Her heart is slower now... she will be fine, she is lucky to have you."

Her mother shakes her head in the steam, "We're blessed to have *you*! All I'm good for is cooking a soup of rags."

He looks away from the mother – lifts the girl's hand and coils a band around her thumb. "Your sorrow is a sign of your love."

She turns, looks from the corner of her eye, "And the food you've left at our door these years past – is that a sign of yours?"

"If I say so, I would be guilty of treason."

"It is a crime?"

"Do you not know? You are an enemy of the party."

The chopsticks scatter on the floor. She faces him, "You are a party member?"

"I once was... I fled and am still running – hiding. But you – why do you not hide? The persecution is ongoing. Christians, especially your kind, are burned in their churches."

"How can a mother hide when her child needs to live?"

"How can a father live when his family starves?"

She turns away, "Thank you for your help. You must go now."

He rises from the sleeping girl's side, "May I visit tomorrow? with things to help?"

She nods, "Only if you will join us for dinner."

"I accept. Please call me Mr. Wòng." He bows – ducks under the clothesline and turns to leave.

She rises before he disappears out the room, "I am called Sister Maleia – and Chúng Fei-Lumeina is my daughter... we thank you, Mr. Wòng."

"I am happy to meet the Chúng Family."

At the Mercy of Music

20 Twin miniature organ pipes whir under the bandages over Lumeina's face. Her breaths peep and cheep into the hollow bath hall. Her mother listens, kneels, feels the chamber hum with song – every puddle, drop, and vapor tingles.

She inhales her daughter's music. She folds her hands, bows her head and exhales lyrics: MISERÉRE MEI, DEUS...

Her flesh absorbs the echo, her skeleton reverberates – ripples her nerves. Her skull catches their song like a water drum catches strikes. Their chant tickles into their bodies, seeks unseen ears, sifts unseen souls. Their chant trickles forth – drips from their fingertips and toes, weaves the still with wind.

She hears her sisters:
SECÚNDUM MAGNAM MISERICÓRDIAM TUAM...

They join her vigil. They draw tears from her eyes – like spider silk drawing dew at sunrise. MISERÉRE MEI...
Droplets cling to her eyelashes – like blood drops swelling from gashes, sprouting feet and crawling her cheeks like lady beetles.

ET SECÚNDUM MULTITÚDINEM MISERATIONUM TUÁRUM –
DELE INIQUITÁTEM MEAM... MISERÉRE MEI...
AMPLIUS LAVA ME AB INIQUITÁTE MEA –
ET A PECCÁTO MEO MUNDA ME... MISERÉRE MEI...
QUÓNIAM INIQUITÁTEM MEAM EGO COGNÓSCO –
ET PECCÁTUM MEUM CONTRA ME EST SEMPER...

They steep in the song – submitting, opening, receiving the water, surrendering their flavor. The spiced bath penetrates – transverberates with every dip into them. The milk seeps in through their pores, fills their flesh, resonates all the way to their marrow.

THE MANY

21 The pipe organ chirps with the morning choir. The damp floor numbs her and leaves her exhausted. She flexes to move but needles pin her muscles in place. Her arm limps aside, loosens and opens itself to fresh blood. She ignores the invisible ants nipping down her limb.

More ants scratch their way to her fingers and toes – their feet prick her.

She ignores them all.

Ducks and other birds squelch the organ. The pipes fall silent. She listens for her daughter's whistles but finds none.

Her eyes widen, she pries herself off the bath hall floor – the ants pinch onto her for dear life. She rises – drops – rises – drops again as blood drips back into her legs.

She peers up and sees Daughter's hair waving – flapping through smog.

A black fuzz hovers and weaves her few strands like frenzied fruit flies. Her mother leaps at them, swings her parched arms, reaches up and lifts her daughter from the hive.

The legion stalks the family.

It murmurs, drones, chases as she carries her still and silent child through the hallways. Daylight flows into the halls – lights their way like beacons.

The swarm pursues – snuffs the sun and dissolves the family into itself, buries them with its little black bodies. She collapses, breaks into a worn wall and crashes to the floor. Mother and child are separated.

She slaps the swarm, shoves it off Lumeina, shouts it off with shrieks. She glances at her daughter's mummy face and searches for her eyes. Two gaping red blotches stare back through the black smoke.

The swarm smears her view and leaps on her child. The murmurs deafen – a cave infested with wasps, thousands of voices groaning. She pulls her hood over her face, shields her eyes, mauls the fumes but misses with every swipe. She swipes on and on – throws her strength away until it leaves her thirsty for breath.

Her hood clings to her mouth – thickens her drink. She casts it off and finds her daughter sleeping in quiet on the floor.

The dust storm is nowhere and the smashed wall is everywhere.

A black pillow of fresh hair cushions Lumeina's head.

BEAUTY SLEEP

22 The shadow is plush. She presses her fingers into the pillow – it conjures lush warm baths with nothing to feel but sighs, summer night skies with nothing to behold but lustrous stars. She runs her hand through the velvet – the dark hair washes her fingers and embraces her hand. It grips her to itself.

She jerks away.

She backs away from her daughter, backs into the wall. She stares at her reflection in the black veil. She remembers Lumeina's hair shedding into the wind, into the tub. She remembers kissing a bald head, bandaging a skinned scalp. She remembers and questions her memory.

She rises and starts down the hallway, finds the steel tub and the rusty water – the still red with a film of delicate skin curdling into congee. She stirs the porridge for kelp but finds none.

She returns to her daughter's side – approaches slow. She touches the little bound brow. The gawky red blotches and squeaky breaths seek her mother. They seek and do not cease.

She raises her child off the floor, cradles her in her lap. She combs Daughter's hair with her hands, slowly until she smiles – stargazes, ponders, wanders.

She wanders the dark forest – swims the dark garden of anemones. The tropical waters flow between her fingers and hold her hands. The shallow reef shimmers with drifting scales and sands. She wades in the shade.

The summer sun heats the home, but the shade cools the family. Sunshine burns through the windows, toasts the floors and walls, crisps the air and broils the ceiling. Hot light crowds out the dark – all the dark but the shade embracing mother and child. Unseen clouds cloak the family from the gaze of day.

"Ah-Neõi... can you hear Ah-Máh? Can you hear me-mah?" she whispers down into her child's hair – her breath trickles along the strands, trickles through the bandages and into her skull. Lumeina's lips blink like eyelids. She feels her mother's heart nudge her head – tap her ear. She knows where she is and sees only what she touches – and only touch through layers of embalming. She smells Mother's whispers. Every word is sweet and her name is safe.

"Ah-Máh very much loves you. Very much cares for you... you are a very beautiful girl – even in this illness, even in these bandages. Lumeina, do not forget your beauty – do not forget God made you... and made you beautiful. Do not forget how all the animals mocked the caterpillar when she was little, when she was a plain and skinny worm. How she tried to grow but only grew fat, how she wept but only trapped herself in her own tears. How God heard her cries but asked her to wait... to trust. And at last, how God made her new – so new she could not remember anything but being true, good and beautiful."

Her mother's words embrace her. Lumeina illustrates her voice – sees the weeping worm, the good God, and the new. She feels fingertips paint crosses over her bandaged brow ✚, over her frayed lips ✚, over her heart ✚.

Mother cups her hand over Daughter's chest – catches her every heartbeat until she sleeps.

FIRST WORD

23 Lumeina stretches out her arm – flexes the wrappings around her muscles, feels them constrict her, restrain her. She makes a fist – stiff bandages snap off her wrist.

She leans away from Mother's nave – leaves room between them for air to cool their sweat. She lifts her head off Mother's arm, pats the ground, walks her fingertips until they find Mother's hand. She tiptoes onto her open palm – she dances ballet.

Her fingertips skate across the sleeping hand, her fingernails etch soft strokes onto Mother's skin. Lumeina traces out the figure she sees in her memory – writes with invisible ink. Red dribbles through her bandages and follows her finger – paves a labyrinth on her mother's hand.

She keeps with the pattern – dances in loops, walks the same path again and again – thickening and bolding the coating. The weight of Lumeina's writing presses down on her mother.

She wakes and sees Daughter tapping on her palm.

A girl's voice tingles into her hand, up her arm, echoes into her body. Her bones resonate. Her ears catch the resonance. She hears:

Ah-Máh?

She splits off the floor, rips her hand away from Lumeina, gasps and stares. Daughter sits up on her shins and bows her head. She reaches up for Mother.

Blood flakes from Mother's palm like dried rice paste. She rubs her hand, brings it to her eyes, sees the fresh red tattoos:

阿媽?

She traces the words – parses them, smells their rusted ink.

She kneels down to Daughter, holds her still and picks the wrappings off the young fingers. She peels the kiwi and finds ripeness. She touches soft skin – sees complexion.

"Ah-Neõi, are you bleeding-mah? Bleeding anywhere?" She searches under the bandages but finds only dried blood blending with sweet sweat.

Lumeina feels her mother's hands pat across her body – crumbling off scabs and crusts. Gone is the legion of lesions.

"How is this possible?" her mother whispers, sits, shakes her head.

Lumeina brushes her fingers over her mother's face, finds her nose, cheeks and lips. She pokes a finger to her cheek and writes into her. Her mother stares at the dumb red blotches and listens: *I don't know... but I know I'm hungry.*

Her daughter's voice sings. It sings and melts her mother into tears.

STRANGE FISH

24 Late autumn leaves shed off her body. A leaf bed piles around her legs – itches and inches up her heels and knees.

Lumeina holds still. She feels Mother guide her hand to her other arm. "Do you feel that?" Mother asks. The bare arm is as soft as warm breath.

Daughter nods. She reaches for her face and picks off the red blots. She stares into the dark – glares at the absence, excavates a path for sight. Her fingernails bite the red earth drooping from her brow. Her thumbs tunnel into the cliff. Mud clogs under her fingernails. The crisp soil moistens and drools down her face.

Mother grips her arms, "Mōh-lah! Don't touch-lah!"

Mother swallows vomit – the seawater burns back into her stomach. Lumeina blinks but her eyelids cling to each other like clot wounds. She struggles to pull away from her mother.

Lumps of flesh seal in her eyes. Fissures mark where eyelids meet – where teardrops leak. Her mother remembers sun dried strawberries – pocked and leathery.

Daughter tries to claw her eye patches off. Mother handcuffs her. Daughter pines to see the day but only sees it through murky red goggles. She stares up to a window – feels the sun stare back, but she only sees thick tomato stew. A bright tomato bobs in the middle.

Lumeina smells tomatoes. She turns to them, shuffles down the hallway and runs to meet them. Her mother chases after her – stomps the trail of husks. She calls for her child – shouts down the throat of the house.

Around the corner, the backdoor claps against the wall. Lumeina kneels beside a bundle of bags, pats them like a sister searching for unseen siblings in their mother's womb.

Her mother joins her on the doorsteps. Lumeina's fingers sprawl over a slip of cardboard – she presses her fingertips into its face. She counts and follows the grooves of pen strokes. Her mother reads over her shoulder as she moves her hand across the note:

Chúng Family – I visited but nobody answered the door. Left these for you – please accept. I will visit again tomorrow.

– Mr. Wòng

Tomato innards spatter the message.

Her mother follows the slime to a hungry mouth with hungry hands doing homage. Lumeina lodges a fruit between her teeth, one in her grip, and presses another to her mother's belly.

She lifts the fruit from her child's hand. Lumeina dives back into the bags and feels a small wall.

She pushes the wall's edges and they splay into a thousand fins. They sweep her fingertips. She remembers how grass sweeps her feet, how Mother's hair sweeps her skin, how her own hair sweeps her body. Lumeina grasps the fins, plucks the strange fish from the sea.

Her mother drops the tomato at first sight of the fresh catch. Gold strokes shimmer like scales in sunny streams:

聖經

"Let Ah-Máh see..." she says, cradles the book's weight. The black binding is chopped like bark. The pages are heavy and crisp with sweat stains.

WANDER GIRL

25 She places her hand where the stain is deepest. She sees all her sisters who held there before – kissed there before.

Lumeina listens to her mother sigh. She rests against her mother's chest and looks with her fingers. Mother guides her touch across the book's terrain: thousands of forests, ponds, creeks, valleys, peaks and paddies under her fingertips.

Her mother reads the landscape aloud, names each new feature. She helps with unclear views – writes on her child's palms, walks her to secret caves and hidden clearings.

She watches Daughter wander. The sacred pages emanate like shavings of sunshine – each turn fans more candlelight into the dark bedroom.

Mother and child dream together.

...

The day without yesterday.

A heart in solitude chants to itself in the black – black as blindness. Its voice seeks ears, its song longs for a beloved. The vast dark ripples in tune – swells forth with words. Its rhythm gathers, bonds and weaves into a wave. The wave hears its will. It bursts into fingers of fire, tearing and searing the dark in two.

The fire sweeps out with colors dripping from its tail – smearing the dark. Blue flows and gushes, pools and hushes into a sea. Brown smacks the waters with applause, then sinks deep – it piles into a bed for the ocean and rises into mountains. Yellow clings to one another and to everything – it melts and glazes all in a glow. White floats and smokes –

breathes as the heart beats. Green speckles, pours and sprouts into limbs and leaves.

Lumeina watches from the dark – tucked atop a warm pillow. She listens to the longing song. She sees the sky birth a twin. The heavier child careens down and buries her – darkens her sight of other colors. The heart's chant helps her forward – beckons her by her bones, taps her spine like fingers to a flute. She kicks off the fallen blues – steps off the cool hues. She swims and rests on the new shores.

The beach succumbs to her steps – adopts the press of her heels and the faces of her toes. The green specks dress the land with lush gowns. Lumeina crouches and catches a patch of lace. It flails its arms – some flap and others clasp her. She pokes the green body and it pops a bud. A stem lifts the bud from the body like a fishing pole. Roots wriggle out between her fingers and reach for the ground.

Lumeina drops the seedling and backs away from its growing arms. Leaves unravel and branches fill the sky like a peacock spreading its tail – engulfing Lumeina in its shade. The tree crowns itself with a headdress of blushing snowflakes. Sea breezes toss the petals into a cloud and swoops low to Lumeina. It bows at her feet and carpets a path ahead. The blossoms cuddle with her every step. She remembers the white ducklings nestling at her feet.

Lumeina turns to the sea and sees where the breeze blew from. Islands of grey flippers and fins leap from the blue – pounce at the sky and smash the ocean into a million shards. Some shards melt away and others skip off together in a shoal. The water warms with little bodies and cities to shelter them. Lumeina gasps as a stretch of coral reef spans out with the waves – unrolls like scrolls of paintings.

The blanket of blossoms ruffles underfoot. She glances down. Feathers lift in all directions – a foamy tsunami lost on land and fleeing into the sky. The wings steal her off her feet. She gives chase – flies along within the cloud of wings, veiled in a womb of down.

The flying flowers escort her to a gateway of genuflecting trees, great and small. The cloud salutes and departs into the wind. Lumeina follows the walkway –

brushes the trees on her left, pats those on her right. They offer her their choicest fruits, they sweeten the air and pucker with nectar and sap.

The kiss of a miniature red heart wins her.

Vines present her with a necklace of the tender rubies – plush and adorned with golden dewdrops. Lumeina dons the gift and tastes that it is good. Each fruit took a breath at birth, held it, saved it – and now they surrender their intimate stash of sky to her lips.

THE TIME OF THE SHADOW

26 Mother sees her daughter's mouth savoring the air –
smiling. Her happy cheeks bulge with each nibble.
She watches Lumeina's cheeks swell and flatten, drool a pink
tint. She dabs the syrup, tastes it off her fingers.

"Strawberry..." she says, pauses and just stands there.
The fruit's fragrance drips from the air like fresh rain.

Pounding rattles the backdoor.

She hurries to the nearest window and peeks across the
courtyard – spies the doorsteps. Her eyes edge up from the
sill like a crocodile. Mr. Wòng lifts his hand, his knocks clap
down the hallway. She rushes against the noise – bashes into
it. The door opens to the day.

"Sister Maleia – good morning. I have more things to
help..."

"Thank you, Mr. Wòng. Please come in – good
morning."

"How is your daughter?"

She says nothing and leads him to the kitchen. He
carries along two swollen bags. She begins to clean, prepare
breakfast. He watches as she finds the words, washes
vegetables, lights the woodstove, wipes her hands.

"Your daughter... has fallen asleep?"

She stops moving.

"Mr. Wòng... do you believe miracles can happen?" She
turns to him but hides her eyes, "Nothing else can explain
it."

Mr. Wòng studies her eyes, her tone, her posture – her
wiry body beneath her burlap, her whisper wrapped in
wonder. She is not like the others.

"Sister – your daughter is well? What do you mean?"
He smells strawberries ripening in the rain.

51

He drops the bags.

Pages flap like frightened ducks, rags wave like laundry in the wind, fruits tumble like avalanche.

Mr. Wòng hears the little fingertip stroke his ribs like a bow to a violin. Her soft echo winds throughout his skeleton and ripples his muscles. He shivers and sighs. He can do nothing but listen: *You saved me – I remember your smell.*

Mr. Wòng turns around and sees a blindfolded girl smiling at him, her fingers brushing his hand. He does not move. Her spotless flesh assaults his sight – challenges his memory of bandaging butchered skin.

He takes the child's hand, bends his knee, crouches to her level. He gazes at her face.

Lumeina sniffs – a strange odor piques her.

Mr. Wòng shakes his head – tries to turn to her mother but cannot.

TOASTED ROSES

27 Their voices drift, sift through the wet summer air and moist wooden walls.

She hears them talk, but the pages speak louder.

The printed text taps her fingertips like a Morse key – a tick and flash, tick and flash – typing on her touch.

Her eyes are wide within their tombs. They follow her wandering hands – tracking like twin spotlights. The story presses her flesh – its image seeps through her fingertips and settles under her fingernails.

Her fingernails – ten little round windows – frame each character as she passes over them. They shimmer like a marquee of magnifying glasses.

...

Mr. Wòng listens to Sister Maleia. He remembers with her – follows while she reenacts the days, shares the evidence. He collects the abandoned bandages, inspects the wounded wall, combs the rusty bathwater, then shakes his head for a long time. He squints – focuses his scrutiny.

"Are you frightened?" Sister Maleia asks.

"No – are you?"

She does not answer.

"I once worked medicine. But nothing here is understandable."

She nods, "And when Lumeina touches – writes... reads... You heard her, didn't you?"

He says nothing. He remembers her voice.

"She's too young... how can she know how?" he says.

"I've barely taught her the basics – but her voice..."

"I've heard ventriloquists before."

53

"She's mute."

Mr. Wòng walks away from Sister. He rubs his face, buries a grin before turning back to her. "Well, if it's not a miracle – I don't know what it is..."

The wooden walls and halls shiver and crackle like a stretching spine – a dragon's spine. Thunder pummels their lungs. Raindrops lash the roof. Sister Maleia rushes to her child.

...

Lumeina does not notice Mother rush in, nor when she calls for her, asks if she is all right. She does not notice when Mr. Wòng and her mother stare at the black brushstrokes beneath her organic glass. They read what she reads, try to pull her hands away from the sacred pages. Her fingers bite onto the binding until her mother tickles her loose. They remove the book.

"Let Ah-Máh and Mr. Wòng see your hands."

Lumeina sniffs out Scripture's worn body. She reaches for it but Mr. Wòng pushes it off. Mother snatches her hands, "Ah-Neõi – did you thank Mr. Wòng for his gifts yet?" Her hands struggle. "Don't be like this-lah."

Mr. Wòng takes a fidgeting hand and guides it to the book, "Lumeina, I'm glad you enjoy reading. You are a very smart girl. But maybe something is wrong with your fingernails... let us look to make sure?"

She raises her arm, extends her hand with regality. They gaze at her peach-opal fingernails, they peer into the crystal and read the mystery.

Her mother rests the book on Lumeina's lap.

"Mr. Wòng, thank you much for returning this."

"Not a problem–" Mr. Wòng stops peering, "it was yours?"

"Yes – how did you come to have it?" Sister Maleia nods. Lumeina nods even more.

Lumeina nods until Mr. Wòng answers. She writes on his arm: *It smells like toasted roses.*

Mr. Wòng bows his head, "I found it after they condemned your house. It was the only thing left. They were burning them."

"How did they miss it – it was on the altar..."

"It was in the bushes when I found it... clinging to a branch like a melon."

Lumeina shakes her head, touches her mother, tries to write, but her mother rises, "Please tell us more over breakfast – I know Lumeina is hungry-loh..."

"Please, don't trouble yourself – I should go now."

"Impossible! Where do you stay? How will you get there? It's storming!" Sister Maleia says. The sky demonstrates her claim – rattles the steel roof with marbles.

First Breakfast

28 They sit on the concrete floor. Tin dishes link them together in between. The cool floor soothes them from the soggy summer breath. A burlap blanket cushions Lumeina.

The Chúng Family's gestures, words and silence are foreign to him. He waits for Sister to invite, but she rests her hands over Lumeina's and his – and just breathes, "Yèh-Sóh... your little sisters thank you for loving us. We thank you for our life, our friends – like Mr. Wòng – and our families. Please bless this meal and bless us – that we may be more like our Mother. Amen." Then, quick taps to their heads, hearts and shoulders ✣. She opens her eyes with a smile. The smile is also foreign to him.

"Breakfast looks tasty," he says.

"I hope it tastes tasty."

It smells tasty!

Lumeina dives in – hands first: *It feels tasty, too!*

They dine together with millions of raindrops aiming to join in.

"Mr. Wòng, I want to thank you again for caring for us – offering so much for us... we've prayed for you for years," Sister Maleia says. Her daughter chews loudly and nods with a hardboiled egg in hand.

"You're both very welcome. I regret Lumeina had to be in danger for me to finally risk coming forward... I'm sorry."

Lumeina reaches for his hand.

They touch.

He watches her little fingers rest. He remembers them peeled and raw only days earlier. The tattoos under her fingernails persist. Sticky rice glues her fingers to him.

"You were telling us about finding the Holy Book..."
Sister says. Lumeina's stomach croaks. She pulls away and
turns back to her meal. Mr. Wòng wanders a moment.

"Yes – it was soon after the party condemned your
house. I saw smoke from where I stayed, followed it and
watched while they tore everything from your rooms and
walls. I'm guessing the book was lucky and fell where they
couldn't see.

"I approached your house a few days after – I was
actually looking for anything to eat. The garden was
unharmed so I picked through it and found the book. I'm still
surprised they didn't burn down the whole house," Mr.
Wòng says. "But I'm even more surprised you came back..."

"I was brought back," she says – puts down her bamboo
sticks. "I remember everything. I don't want to – but I do...
Mr. Wòng – how much do you know about what happened?"

"About... the persecution?"

Sister nods, "Ah-Neõi... do you want to go read some
more?"

Lumeina scurries to her feet, bows goodbye and hurries
off with another egg in her hands. Her mother leads her
across the hall. The girl's long hair is a shadow trailing close
behind.

Sister soon returns.

"Please tell me all you know... I must know."

The marbles fall in stampedes across the roof –
stomping the roof into rust.

ONE HUNDRED FLOWERS

29 "The party was deceptive when it granted freedom for religion to emerge and grow. It invested years of patience and tolerance to convince the underground to surface. The last kind to accept the party's open arms was yours – and even then it was already decades into the party's new policy.

"No one knew the party's intentions – but looking back they knew what they were doing, knew what they wanted and how to get it.

"I don't know the intention but can guess it was fishing hook. They wanted to draw all religious people out even to see who would eventually become religious. They allowed every religion to show in safety, to convert neighbors, and to live in the public. They accommodated, hosted, encouraged and even financed. They opened to all foreigners to visit and aid. The more religions that came forward, the happier the party appeared. They were inspired by the old One Hundred Flowers campaign... and they made great effort trying to have people forget what had happened to their great, great grandparents..."

"China forgot..."

"And the party never forgot.

"They wanted to purge the Middle Kingdom – wanted her to vomit God from her gut. They did not imprison, reeducate, or deport – those were grave errors they were determined never to repeat. They sought more permanent and assured success.

"Sister Maleia... I am almost certain you and your child are the sole survivors of your kind. The party especially despised you – your kind was their main target. They neve forgot what that old Polish man did to their brother parties in Europe.

"Sister – I know it will be difficult, but you and your daughter must leave here before it is too late. You are young, healthy enough to run. It is impossible for the party not to discover you here, even though they appear to have not... believe me – there is always intention."

The rain fills the silence left by Mr. Wòng. Lightning slaps the windows with white paint. Sister waits for the thunder to pass.

"She's too young."

"She will lose her youth – and more – if you stay."

"Mr. Wòng... there is always intention."

"Forgive me for caring too much, but miracles don't last forever."

"I don't rely on miracles."

"But she relies on you."

"And I rely on God."

"How can God be in this place? He has abandoned you to the party."

"Mr. Wòng – you are our friend and welcome here. But you are wrong – it is we who have abandoned God." Sister Maleia rises and leaves the kitchen. Her footsteps disappear across the hall.

Mr. Wòng shakes his head – shakes off a grin. He sighs with the thunder, "This will be interesting..."

BECAUSE OF BEAUTY

30 The pump screeches while Mother milks the well. Lumeina sways with the waves – bobs against the steel tub. She scoops water to her head and shivers – the cool handful tingles down. Her mother holds her, fills the pail. Lumeina waits – braces for the cold douse.

The wood boat bumps her belly.

The rain is loud in the bath hall.

Lumeina hunches under the cold water. The Ark tumbles away. She clenches the water and shakes her fists. Her mother rinses her long hair – the strands float around her, soften her seat.

"What are you thinking about, Ah-Neõi?"

Lumeina swims her fingers through her drifting hair. Her hands are schools of fish and shoals of jellies.

Mother sponges her right arm, eyes the kiwi seed nestled under her skin. She rubs the mole on Daughter's wrist, stares into its pupil, holds her own arm beside her child's. The two eyes – one a bit bigger than the other – meet hers.

Lumeina traces on her mother's arm: *Did Ah-Bàh make it flood so much because he likes fish?*

"No..."

Does he like whales?

"Not only whales... Ah-Bàh loves all his creatures."

Even the bad ones?

"Mmm hmm! He especially loves you... you are his dream come true."

But my eyes are ugly now.

Her mother sniffles. She tastes seawater drip to her lips, "No... he's making your eyes better – more beautiful."

He can do that?

"Ah-Bàh *will* do that. He will make all things new..."

Her mother removes her blindfolds. The loosening bands fall away – leaving an itch crowning her head. Mother draws water from a separate pail, sprinkles the clot eyelids. The lesions drool sputum like bruised lips, like rusty honeycombs. The shower washes away the crown.

"Ah-Neõi... Ah-Máh wants to know why you went outside – Ah-Máh told you not to... Outside is very dangerous..." she whispers and offers her palm.

Because I wanted to feel it.

"Feel what?"

Beauty.

"What was beautiful?"

Everything.

Mother stops asking.

They listen to the rain. Distant thunder growls – the noise shudders the air, prickles Lumeina's skin. She knows the sound and has felt the feeling.

Is Ah-Bàh hungry?

Mother kisses her forehead, helps her out of the tub, swathes her in a dry rag, "*Ah-Bàh* is always hungry. He loves our prayers the most – let's go give him some..."

...

The chapel trickles with droplets clapping the floor. Lumeina follows Mother with one hand and holds a candlestick with the other. The family kneels before the empty womb in the wall. She smells toasted roses wafting from above.

She leans up. Her mother begins to hum. Lumeina tiptoes with her knees, stiffens her legs and kneecaps, tilts her nose to the nook, reaches for the aroma. Her brow barely reaches past her mother's breast.

SERENUS

31 Her head nudges her mother's shoulder. The toasted roses are stale – leeched dry of fragrance. Her nine-year-old body presses her calloused knees into the floor. Lumeina catches her drooping head – jerks back like a marionette. Her mother pats her nape – massages. She fights a yawn – bites unseen hands pulling down her jaw.

Her fingers limp along the knotted cord.

They close night prayer with a bow. Her mother carries her to bed, hums a lullaby that calms the house.

...

The song longs for a beloved. The chant wraps its resonance with good land. Its heartbeat warms its robe into flesh, its heart folds and fits within its chest. Lumeina listens to the rhythm focus, then dampen behind a breast. She knows the song.

She drops the plush ruby from her hands. The berry's blood hatches and seeds the soil. Lumeina skips off, rushes down the walkway, passes all the great trees with their arms raised and full of harvest.

A spring rests in a clearing. Gems pave the water's route throughout the lush. The water is sweet with warmth and warm with sweetness.

The garden opens to her. Curtains of blossoms, fruits and leaves turn aside for her steps. She wanders the gift. Her flesh feasts on the life embracing her presence. She breathes and everything sighs. She sighs and everything breathes. A veil makes way for her. She passes through.

She stops. She brushes her hair from her eyes. She gazes upon the man. She gazes from behind.

He stands before her – pure, strong and fresh. The kingdom of creation stands before him – under him. He listens to the hearts of all the animals – tries to sing with them. Lumeina hears his chant search every bird and beast – all creatures from west to east. She gazes while he seeks.

...

The sun bows to the moon – tucks its face in night. The man rests on a bed of flowers and sleeps within deep dreams. The song in his heart serenades his fantasy. Lumeina watches his breaths lift his chest and empty, lift and empty – his ribs are like fingers massaging his heart.

She keeps vigil with the stars.

...

The moon bows to the sun – shrouds its brow in day. The clouds blush from violet to papaya. White huddles around the yolk. Lumeina waits for sunshine to stroke the man – its hands reach close to his heart, break off its stem and plant it with the flowers.

The stem remains warm and resonant with his song. Petals of all flavors bloom from its marrow, trickle up to his ear and down to his ankle. The blossoms repose at his side – hold him like a blanket.

His blanket kisses – feels his bones with hers. He rouses from sleep. He casts aside mere dream and leaps to his knees – kneels before his dream lying beside him. His body blushes, his blood trills and his heart hears his beloved's – and her heart hears hers.

The woman rises from her bouquet bed. She sits, smiles and laughs while the man's body dances to her song. The man and woman dance the day away to their song.

AZARIAS

32 The boys pick at the soil – their calloused feet strike the coarse land like matchsticks. A kite with a life leads them down a pimpled dirt road. Their worn shirts cling to their wet skin.

"Don't let it escape-ah!"

"It's getting tired-lah!"

The five boys spit at the floating tissues – slathering them with battle cries. The black flakes flutter in the summer sun like burnt paper. Gold and silver pollen embroiders the dark leaves like cooling embers.

Tall wild weeds enclose the road in a narrow sleeve. The walls of long grass billow and gush like a parted sea. The butterfly climbs – crawls out of the tunnel and swims over the waves. The boys dive in pursuit, peek up as they push through the thicket like submarines. They leave flattened trails behind them – paths of downed stalks thrice their height. They carve the field's blank face.

"I bet I'll catch it first!"

"I bet you can't!"

The grass separates the group – beckons each to shape his own maze. The youngest one – the quietest, thinnest and smallest boy cuts his way quicker than the others. He slips between the weeds, skips over dips, stalks the mini manta. His modest dent helps him hide in the depths.

A dense reef snags him in its snares. He struggles through the bamboo patch – squeezes through narrow gaps, bends his arms, legs and back like an octopus.

He falls off the edge of the world.

The open land swallows him in day. His arms flail, his legs fumble, and he gawks at the house nestled in a garden framed with fluffed paddies.

Cirrus-white ducks squeal at his stumbling feet. They smack the wind and climb the sky. He waits for them to flee. He waddles away from their nest and listens to the quiet house.

Patrolling the perimeter is a squad of guards – a pineapple palisade. The plants stand their ground and hold their ripe heads high above their arms – dozens of arms each with gleaming sword in hand. The wind buffs their jade blades.

A shadow fades in over the pineapples and then ahead. The butterfly hops overhead and perches on wildflowers. The boy watches it rest. It folds its wings into a card, opens then shuts them like a little mouth. He nears the black kite with soft steps – his feet sweep the earth with shy strides.

He pounces. Hands cupped into a cage.

He lands. Dust erupts about him.

The butterfly sneaks off in the smokescreen. The boy dives and prowls.

He tracks the wings through the garden and to the doorsteps. The butterfly perches again, on the top step, before slipping from sight. The dark doorway and the dark hallway cloak the dark wings. He squints his eyes, focuses his stare.

Bright embroidery reveals its distant constellation.

The boy crouches and shuffles into the hallway. His feet smudge the floor with sand and plucked grass. The splintered walls box him in and draw him deep into the body. He follows the stars in the dark, waits for his eyes to accept the night.

He speeds up – grips the concrete with his toes, closes in on the shimmers. He twists around a corner, bursts into a wide room.

He freezes.

Novas explode into view. Dust glitters in streaks of color. Painted clouds hover in and out of shade. He stands where sun spills through stained windows. He drowns in the gems and does not struggle.

Then he sees her.

His heart begins to chant.

She turns around.
It sings.
She hears his.

BLIND BEAUTY

33 He hears hers.
The stained sunshine highlights her in snow, blush and candlelight.

The taller woman leads the little woman along. Their gritty gowns guard them from what he wants them to be guarded from. He gazes at the girl and finds her eyes enshrined behind shields. His heart sings for the seals to part. His heart knocks and keeps watch.

"Hello?" the woman says.

His heartbeat muffles her voice. He bows his head as the family approaches.

"Do you need help, young man?"

He glances to the woman, then back to the girl. He stays with her.

"Who are you?" he asks.

"I am Sister Maleia – my daughter can't speak..." her mother says. He steps closer to the girl – sees her little nose wrinkle and sniffle, her face swaddled in bandages. He wanders her black hair, peers past her bangs and into the willow grove.

She touches him – her fingers to his ear. She strokes the sepals, follows the lobe to his cheek: *I am Fei-Lumeina. Who are you?*

The boy skips a breath and gasps. Her fingerprints rub his skin – he feels her every crease pluck him like piano string. A warm phantom touch sleeps on his cheek. The sweat from her hand soothes and seeps. He sighs his reply, "I am Fàn Yíng..." he pauses, "my friends call me Little Yíng..."

His voice vibrates along his teeth, through his cheek, into her fingers.

Lumeina smiles.

He watches her giggle – her lips undress her teeth. He remembers peeling ripe mangosteens. He smells the fruit in her excited breaths.

"Are we friends now?" Little Yíng asks.

Lumeina nods.

He reaches for her hand and hugs it in his palm.

"Hungry-mah, Little Yíng? Will you have lunch with us?" her mother says. He follows them out and the butterfly wades in viscid sunshine.

LIBRARY

34 Little Yíng listens to her chew: her lips smack, her tongue lathers, her cheeks muffle the clicks of her teeth. He hears her throat embrace each bite, hears her belly ripple with sprinkling rice. He eats slow, breathes slower and wonders why she sounds so new.

Lumeina's mother smiles. She refills her daughter's tin dish with lumps of rice – steam rises like wisps of cotton.

"Not hungry-méh? Little Yíng?" her words take time for him to hear. His stomach answers before him. He gathers more fried egg between his chopsticks. "Have more-mah?"

He nods.

"Little Yíng... how old are you-lah?"

"Almost ten..."

"Oh? You're not so little-lah! Lumeina also is nine!"

"I'm little because my friends are bigger," he says. He falls quiet – falls back into her song.

"Little Yíng, what are you thinking about-ah?" her question takes even more time.

"I don't know... lots of things..."

Lumeina reaches for her mother and scribbles with rice-paste fingers: *Can we go play after lunch?*

"Only if you stay inside the house – and only if Little Yíng doesn't leave hungry."

Lumeina stretches to touch her new friend. He meets her halfway with an open hand.

Eat more so we can go play!

He packs his face – it swells into a potato, his belly into a plump squash.

...

Lumeina leads Little Yíng by the hand. He follows her through the halls to a room. Her bare feet feel for grooves chiseled into the floor, her hand feels him sweat into hers. Little Yíng watches her swift steps turn with the grooves – dancing with them. They stop at a doorway with words carved into the floor. She takes a deep breath – smells. He reads the shallow engraving with his finger:

图書館

He does not look up until she tugs him inside.

Book spines line the room's walls like scales on a crocodile's underbelly. The aged pages sigh the odor of stale bread. Lumeina hurries to a wall and presses her friend's palm to the worn spines. She strokes the back of his hand – rolls her fingertips over his tendons and knuckles: *See anything you like?*

Little Yíng slides his hand over the underbelly. Titles and titles cascade up and down the wall. His eyes tumble in their sockets, zipping from one to another. She nudges a book to his chest. The cover stares at him. He stares back at its foreign face.

"You can read this?" He opens the book.

She nods – reaches for the words and gathers them with her fingers.

"It looks strange..."

It's English. It taught me how Ah-Bàh makes animals. There are pictures.

Lumeina flips the pages until a heavy leaf smacks her fingers. He looks as her hand takes in the view of a jungle crawling with animals. Her thumb traces creatures with stretched necks, others with talons for teeth, and ones with jaws bigger than their heads.

"Who taught you English?" Little Yíng asks.

I don't know – I always knew. You don't know it?

"Can you teach me?" He glances at the collection – more foreign faces appear. They emerge from the Chinese crowd, sneak into sight like guerilla agents. He brings her hands to their lips – she feels them speak. They swing from one face to another:

This is: *latina,*
français,
ελληνικά,
한국어,
tiếng Việt,
italiana,
קלאס תעברית,
日本語,
ру́сский,
español,

العربيــة,
Kiswahili,
Polski,
پنجـــابى,
Diné bizaad,
Filipino,
Afrikaans,
slovenčina,
português,
and ⠿

Little Yíng's hands are weary. "Where did these books come from-gah? I didn't know there were so many languages... amazing..." he releases her hands. She comes to his face – brushes her fingertips along his brow, his eyelashes. Little Yíng does not blink.

Amazing...

Little Yíng brings his fingers to her hair trickling past her ear. His sweat glosses her black strands. Lumeina feels him gaze.

Do you see something?

He moves to the fringes of her bandages. Pink stains reveal the swelling beneath.

"Do your eyes hurt?" he asks.

No. It itches sometimes. I'm not allowed to scratch.

"What happened?"

Mr. Wòng said the sun was too strong. I miss the sun.

"Is he your father?"

No. He's our friend. He saved me from the sun.

Lumeina's head perks up. She hops and pulls Little Yíng along. They scamper through the hallways. She stops suddenly at the chapel doors, falls to her knees and bows. She waits for Little Yíng. He waits for her.

They wait for each other.

Little Yíng lowers himself to the floor – folds himself down like her. He reads the new engravings:

小教堂

He rises when she does.

Lumeina leads her friend to the box in the wall and peers up – her hands clasped over her heart. Her stillness and silence remind him of clouds in a quiet sky. He follows her gaze to a skeleton of mangled wire and shrapnel drooping from two beams of wood fixed together like a giant *ten*:

✝

"Fei... what is that?" Little Yíng asks. She strikes the floor with her right knee, her hands move in a blur ✝, then she stands and reaches for the book nestled above. She lifts it from the box. She coddles it.

I hear him in here.

"Hear who?"

Ah-Bàh.

"Who?"

My father.

Little Yíng looks – gasps. The butterfly lolls on the cover – asleep with limp wings and legs. He touches Fei – stops her with his whisper. Her hand nears the creature. She notices its weight on the book.

The wings flash, the legs flinch, the butterfly lifts off. Little Yíng leaps up with frenzy – pecks the air with his fingers, but the wings grace upon Lumeina's hair. Its black body and silk wings crown her with a headdress. Its shy feet pinch her strands – kiss her like a breath.

"It's the butterfly!" Little Yíng says. "It led me here."

It tickles!

They smile. They sit and read together and laugh when the wings flit from Fei to Little Yíng, to the book's pages, back to Fei. It shrouds them in a nimbus of pollen. Their laughter echoes in the chapel – cheeps throughout the house.

NIGHT COVER

35 Her mother tracks the giggles to the chapel. She peeks inside and watches the children dance in the aisle – the butterfly hovering just above their reach. Her daughter claps her hands and feet. Little Yíng crouches and springs into the air. They do not notice her approaching.

She raises her hand over their heads – stands like a statue. The children become still. The air settles. Little Yíng watches the butterfly circle overhead, then perch on Sister Maleia's palm.

"It was afraid of you... you must be gentle..." her mother brings the wings to their level. "Should we feed it? It must be hungry for dinner by now... just like you two!"

The children nod.

As they leave the chapel, Little Yíng glances back – eyes the black book in the gold nook. His gaze stops at the mangy mass sagging from the beams. He sees the man. The late afternoon sun sets the skeleton on fire.

...

The kitchen floor is crowded with warped sheets of tin. Their meal shines off the metal scraps.

Little Yíng mimics the family's nimble gestures ✞ – memorizes Lumeina's motions and her mother's words over the food.

The butterfly suckles fruit peels on a tin nearby.

They begin to eat.

"Little Yíng – you must eat quickly. It'll be dark soon... your parents will worry."

"My parents went away-loh."

"Oh – where did they go?"

"To the city for work. I stay with their friends."

"When will they come home?"

"Don't know. I don't even remember when they went."

"Still, you should return soon – don't worry others for no reason."

"Yes... Sister Maleia..." Little Yíng pauses, "why do I call you *sister*? Are you my sister?"

"I'll explain next time you visit..." she smiles. Lumeina taps in:

Tomorrow! Visit again tomorrow!

"Little Yíng may visit anytime as long as his parents' friends allow – all right? Little Yíng?"

He nods.

"Is your village far from here?"

"A little – we only went this far because we wanted to catch the butterfly."

"You and your friends?"

He nods, "I followed the butterfly here. I don't know where they went..." he shrugs.

"Do you want to take the butterfly with you?" her mother asks. Little Yíng looks to it, then shakes his head.

"No – it will be safe here, with you." he says. Her mother leans close to him.

"Little Yíng... this sounds strange, but we need your help to keep this place secret. We are hiding from dangerous people who don't like us... can you keep us secret?" her mother says.

"Dangerous people?"

"Many of them... please keep us secret, Little Yíng..."

He sees Lumeina bite her lip and bow her head. Her mother touches him on the hand.

"I will keep you secret – forever."

...

Lumeina wraps her arms around him before letting him go. He memorizes her: her coarse gown, her lank black hair, her mangosteen lips and teeth, her blotched eyes. Sister Maleia kisses him on the head and pats his shoulder.

"Goodnight Sister Maleia, Fei-Lumeina..." he says.

Lumeina smiles and touches: *I like when you call me Fei.*

"Fei..." he repeats.

Follow the butterfly if you forget your way!

Little Yíng nods and heads off – down the steps, through the garden, over the fields, around the duck nest, past the pineapple palisade, and into the bamboo reef bordering the sea. He climbs into the thicket and sits until nightfall – until nothing can see him emerge onto the dirt road.

He touches where Fei touched him last.

He holds her hand all the way home.

BOYS

36 Little Yíng hears the other boys cap their jars, knock their glasses together like beer bottles. Green puffs tumble in the jars. The boys shake the fireflies until they clink like ice cubes. The bulbs burn out.

"Yíng-Yíng! Is that you?" a boy shouts.

Little Yíng recognizes their silhouettes against the free-roaming fireflies.

"Where did you go? Did you catch the butterfly-mah?" the boy shouts again.

"No – it got away."

The boys laugh. They take their turns at Little Yíng:

"Looks like you're still the only one who hasn't!"

"It's only a butterfly-jeh!"

"We even caught dragonflies today!"

Little Yíng just gazes ahead of them – watches the lightning bugs embroider the night, like the wings that dressed her hair, her hair that he wandered in.

He stargazes.

"Yíng-Yíng! What are you staring at-ah?"

"Are you listening to us?"

They shove him off his feet.

"You look like you saw the devil!"

Little Yíng grits his teeth – shakes his head like a fist. "No!" He gets up, "If I saw the devil I would be dead-lah!"

"You still didn't say where you went all day!" the oldest boy says, "and what's wrong with your arm?"

Little Yíng releases Fei. Her phantom touch dissipates – dissolves like the tingle of a mosquito's footwork on his skin. "I don't know, Dài Mòu – I think I fell and blacked-out. When I opened my eyes it was already dark-loh."

They gawk at his excuse.

"Stupid Yíng-Yíng!"

"Hurts himself chasing a butterfly-jeh!"

"We waited for you all day-lah! Wasted our day-lah!"

"I'm sorry – sorry Dài Mòu..."

"Come on! Now we can go home-lah – without my mom killing us! I'm so hungry-lah!" Big Mòu snatches Little Yíng and drags him. The other boys run off snickering, shaking their jars of broken lights.

HEART TO HEART

37 Lumeina rests beside her mother on the blankets. Mother presses her nose and lips to Daughter's hair, inhales, then sighs. She remembers the subtle scent of approaching rain – a sea breeze stranded in the sky. Lumeina remembers the butterfly's feet.

"Little Yíng is a very kind boy," her mother says.

Daughter nods slow. Mother's breath tickles.

"Do you like him, Ah-Neõi?"

Very much.

"Me too..."

I miss him.

She feels her mother's lips curl into a smile – parting her hair at its roots. "What do you miss most about him?" she asks, waits for Lumeina.

Him.

Mother's smile widens. She dampens Lumeina's hair with giggles. "Hmm... do you want to learn how to make butterflies-mah? for Little Yíng?"

Her daughter turns to face her.

Make butterflies? Yes!

"Ah-Máh will teach you tomorrow – good-mah?"

How do I make tomorrow come faster?

"Sleep earlier... close your eyes-lah... let Ah-Bàh dream a new day for you..."

My eyes are already closed.

"Not only those eyes – your eyes in here, too..." she pats her child's heart, "and in your soul."

How?

"Pray with Ah-Máh, for Little Yíng to be very strong..."

They take a long string of knots into their hands, share the rosary beads, join the crickets with their whispers.

PAPERWORK

38 Newspapers mask the floor around them. Long drawn sips – sip... sip... sip... echo in the calm kitchen. Mother and Daughter huddle beside each other with their sleeves rolled up.

The paper submits to her fingertips – bows its body to her. Lumeina switches from her square, feels for changes in her mother's work, makes creases to her own until it ceases being different. She chases her mother's steps.

"Màhn-māhn-lèi... slowly-lèi – not so fast... beautiful work takes time..."

Newspaper ink grouts her fingerprints and nails. It smudges the creases – tints the paper's wrinkles into black veins. The vessels crawl the paper and fill its wings with blood. Lumeina senses the rigid lacework in its body – under its crisp skin. She spreads her hands and reads its fortune.

Mother takes her hands and guides her through the next steps: twisting, tucking, pushing, pressing and stretching the animal to life. They bend joints into its bones, massage muscles onto its skeleton, press their sweat into its thirsty husk, flex and rig tendons through its flesh. They rouse it from slumber – Lumeina blows the dust off its grey face.

The two butterflies meet on her palm – their weight like plucked petals. Her breath tilts their tattooed wings. Lumeina smirks and sniffs. She smells chalk waft from their wobbling bodies.

"Do you like them-mah?" her mother asks. Lumeina bobs her head.

Not as good as Ah-Bàh's – but not bad.

Mother laughs, "No one can make things like Ah-Bàh can..."

No, but you can!

"What do you mean?"

You made me!

"Oh! But Ah-Bàh helped a lot..." she laughs – kisses her daughter's hair, "and he's still helping..."

Lumeina leans up and nudges her mother's chin.

You smell sweet.

"You smell sweeter, Ah-Neõi..."

When I grow up, I want to be just like you.

"You be a saint – be much better than Ah-Máh."

Better? But how?

"Ah-Bàh and Ah-Máh always will help you – always."

Lumeina tucks a butterfly under her hair and the other under Mother's coif.

Help me make more?

"More butterflies? or other things?"

Both!

LAUGHING ALONE

39 Lonesome laughter stops Mr. Wòng at the doorsteps. The giggles smack him and tickle his straight face. He sets down a plastic bag of rags. He steps in and follows the scents and sounds to the kitchen.

He arrives.

The giggles stop.

Dozens of little bodies branded with Chinese characters guard the kitchen. Grey frogs clutter the floor – chain off entry and are poised to pounce on trespassers. A fence of albino giraffes stand sentry along the way. They peer over and into the distance. Behind them are roaring wads of newspaper arrayed with hooves, jaws and claws.

Sister Maleia snarls with a little lion in her hands – she nudges its paper mane against Lumeina's sole. The girl quivers with mute laughter – tries to curl away from the wild animals surrounding her. She mashes and casts aside the paper predators. Her mother laughs for both of them – the girl's giddy body resounds through her mother's.

Mr. Wòng watches from the hallway, his rough face cracks with each chuckle.

Sister scoops Lumeina into her lap and attacks her armpits with a giraffe. Her daughter drinks air – prepares to scream but only smiles, trembles in silence. Her arms wring her mother's waist. She grabs her mother's hand, scribbles a frenzy: *No more! Stop!!!*

Her mother sits back. Lumeina rolls to the floor and shakes out the last crumbs in her lungs. Mr. Wòng just smiles. He waves when Sister notices him.

"Mr. Wòng! Welcome to Lumeina's Zoo!"

"Thank you! Do I need an admission ticket?"

"Don't know – ask the zoo master..." She nods to her daughter.

Lumeina sprawls on her back and shakes her head. Mr. Wòng leans down and checks her bandages with a pat. She keeps still.

He pats again.

"Hurt-mah?"

She shakes her head. Her arms spring around him like a bear trap. He picks her up, "Good! Very good!" He brushes his fingers through her hair, "Do you want to show me your animals, Little Miss Zoo Master?" He swings her to his side, reaches for a set of smashed stilts. Lumeina takes and mends. The animal's fur is a patchwork of old Hong Kong celebrity headlines. She ignores the ink.

This is a long-neck deer.

"Really?" Mr. Wòng says.

"Tell Mr. Wòng why Ah-Bàh made their necks and legs so long..." her mother says.

To make me laugh!

"Why do they make you laugh?"

They're so funny looking! How do they sleep?

He smiles, watches Lumeina tug the giraffe's legs, "I'm not sure!" He spots a mound of paper bubbles nearby. The inflated paper balloons remind him of sliced carambola. He gathers the puffed stars and brings them to the master. Her mother grins.

"You need an aquarium for all these starfish..." Mr. Wòng drops the newspaper puffs into her small hands – pours them like a handful of soybeans. Her face breaks into a mute squeal.

These aren't starfish! It's elephant poop!

Lumeina squirms – tosses the feces into his face. The clumps scatter. He shuts his eyes at the flung dung.

When he opens his eyes, Sister Maleia flicks a row of stars from her palm. She aims another row at her daughter and friend.

They return fire and declare war.

ORIGAMI WAR

40 "Surrender! Or there will be no lunch!" Sister calls out from behind a fortress of newspaper boulders.

"It is *you* who must surrender... or *no one* will eat your lunch!" Mr. Wòng counters. He and Lumeina huddle outside the doorway with a stack of raw artillery between them. He can only see Lumeina's little toes poking from behind the newspaper pile.

The battlefield is strewn with grey animal carrion: polar bear pelts, zebra strips, panda chunks, and dung trails left by fleeing stampedes. Mortar shells, landmine clusters and downed missiles rest among the dead on the kitchen floor and hallway.

"More lunch for me then!" Sister Maleia laughs.

"We'll see about that! You're outnumbered!"

Lumeina does not hear their war cries. Condemned to create – she kneels over her papier-mâché of squares and sweat, her fingers black and wet. A massive army of air power accumulates beneath her wings. Dozens of species of butterfly spring from the loins of her fingers – each with an arsenal of paper stars ready to launch and drop.

The battle cries cease. Mr. Wòng leans up, peeks over the newspaper wall and spies Lumeina's airbase operations. He stares at the nest of butterflies resting on a bed of stars.

Without turning away, he waves his hand at her mother.

Sister sees the white flag and sneaks over with a paper wad behind her back. The wad limps away when she sees the nest. Together, they stare at the little creator – they follow the blur of her nimble hands and fingers.

...

Her mother sits beside the nest. She watches butterflies being born by the minute. Mr. Wòng lifts one to his eye and inspects: "You taught her all these?"

"No... I only know three styles. I've never seen these before..."

"Incredible..."

"Ah-Neõi... these butterflies are all for Little Yíng-méh?"

Lumeina nods.

"Little Yíng? Who's that?"

"He's Lumeina's new friend – a very sweet boy from the village nearby."

Mr. Wòng's face tightens.

She watches his eyes widen, "Don't worry... we told him to keep us secret – we trust him."

Mr. Wòng motions her to follow him down the hall. Newspapers shuffle under their feet like flowing sea surf. They stand at the backdoor – their conversation a whisper. Mr. Wòng starts, "He's only a child? Was he alone?"

"Yes... what's the matter?"

"Sister – you *know* you and your daughter are enemies of the party... it's very dangerous."

"We talked this over before-loh..."

"I know, I know – you trust God... but even God doesn't want you to be this naïve. If others learn about you from the boy – if that happens..."

"Mr. Wòng... Lumeina needs friends besides us." She holds his hands in hers, "Little Yíng is the answer to my prayer all these years – I asked for him..."

"Méh?" he shakes his head, "I want to talk to the boy – what does he look like?" He watches Sister smile. Her arm reaches outside and waves.

"Like him!" she says – welcomes the shy child waiting in the garden.

FIRST IMPRESSION

41 "Hello Sister Maleia," Little Yíng says with a bow. He turns to the man, "Are you Mr. Wòng?"

"Yes – how did you know?"

"Ah-Fei told me about you. Thank you for saving her."

From behind Sister and Mr. Wòng, a rush of applause welcomes Little Yíng. They turn and see Lumeina racing down the hallway – her feet clapping the floor like a basilisk lizard's over water. Her hair trails her like a banner. They watch her leap outside and swallow Little Yíng in a hug.

"Ah-Luu!" he yelps.

She rubs his name onto his back – her fingertips traverse the peaks of his spine and the valleys between his ribs.

Little Yíng! I missed you!

"I missed you too!"

Luu clasps his hand and rushes him inside. They vanish down the hallway and into the nest of newspapers.

"How long since they first met?" Mr. Wòng asks. His eyes stare down the tunnel.

"Almost one day," Sister smiles. "I think she fascinates him as much as she fascinates you..."

"I think he fascinates *her* even more..." he says, turns to Sister Maleia. Her young face is bright in the sun. Fine strands of black sprout from beneath her burlap coif – veiling her in soft shadows. He forgets her age and sees her daughter.

She notices him gazing, "What are you looking at?"

He closes his eyes – blinks and remembers, "Sister – there's something I never told you about the village..."

She listens.

"When I came here years ago – after your community was taken... the village was vacant. I walked through the town and heard nothing – saw no one.

"The state had confiscated the village, removed the residents and planted new residents – the migrants. It was to prevent dissidence from spreading among the floating population."

"Méh?" Sister says.

"The party not only wanted to rid the nation of your kind, but also of your sympathizers. The party knew what the blood of martyrs would do."

"How do you know this?" she says.

"I helped them."

Her eyes freeze in their sockets. The shadows on her face thicken.

"I tried to tell you all these years... but I knew how close your community was to the villagers. I didn't know how to say it."

"But why are you telling me now?"

"Because of Little Yíng – he must be a child of those migrants. They cannot be trusted – they must not be... they are too indebted to the party."

She looks away and into the house. The children's silhouettes dance in the distance. She turns back to Mr. Wòng, "If it frightens you – I will understand if you leave us..."

Mr. Wòng stands straighter, "No! It doesn't frighten me. It's not about me."

"If it is about Lumeina–"

"It is!"

"Then let her mother care for her. I know you care too – and I cannot stop you. Thank you for that..."

"She needs a father–" Mr. Wòng stops himself.

Sister searches his face.

"She has one – one who has not given us any reason to distrust him yet."

"Your faith is absurd." He looks her in the eye.

"And *you* are absurd for saying that... as if you could've seen where you are now back when you joined the party and

sang its anthem by heart." Her fingernail cuts into his chest –
jousts where his pulse is loudest.

He stumbles from the jabs of her finger.

"If you care about her, then meet the friend God made
for her. You might come to love him as much as you've come
to love the archenemies of your party."

SPELUNKERS

42 Little Yíng and Luu rake the kitchen floor with their hands and feet – gathering the origami bodies and grey leaves. He sorts the scraps into a stack – lays sheet upon sheet like pages of a phonebook. She tends the paper pets – herds them into a flock and sends them to pasture in another room.

Mr. Wòng scoops the stars and fills them into plastic bags. The bags ruffle like static in his grip. The noise reminds Little Yíng of scouring radio channels. Fei reminds him of a song.

"Little Yíng – do you like the butterflies Lumeina made for you?"

"I like them very much! She told me you taught her."

"Only a few... most of them she invented on her own!"

"So creative... where did you learn to fold them-geh?"

"From my sisters – I had a lot of them! They all knew a few... so together they knew a lot!"

"Will you teach me too?"

"Sure! But it seems Lumeina is more talented than me now... better if you ask her..."

Little Yíng sorts the last scraps and hurries out to seek his teacher. He bounds off with the phonebook. Sister turns to Mr. Wòng and raises her eyes at him. She turns back to the boiling potatoes.

"Fine... he's a good boy, but don't say I didn't warn you and your God." Mr. Wòng says. She shrugs and snuffs out the wood stove.

"That's good enough for me." she says. He watches the steam blush her cheeks and darken her veil. He turns to the worn kitchen window and searches his reflection – reads his age.

"I want to ask – why did you decide to become a sister?"

She smiles his way, "I thought you would never ask... I'll tell you over the meal – Little Yíng wants to know too."

Mr. Wòng leaves to call for the children while she sets the floor.

Something stops him.

She spots him in the hallway – frozen in awe of something, staring away. She hears Little Yíng laughing and snow drifting.

She pokes her head from the kitchen door like a tortoise.

A wall of sleeping butterflies dams the hallway. More tumble into the hall with every giggle and quiver. Her mother nears the landslide and starts digging, "Lumeina? Little Yíng?"

"We're in here!" he laughs. Wings burst from where he waves his hand. Her mother plunges into the ashen snow – diving in until it swallows her whole.

Mr. Wòng just stares.

Her mother burrows through the crinkles and curls – peers through gaps between the wings. Butterflies hem her from all sides. She homes in on the children's den.

A grotto opens up with her daughter enshrined in its womb. The little sunlight that drips into the cave shines along her hair – brightens the lair. Dust lingers in the air like kindled pollen. Luu finishes another creation and wiggles her fingers within its wings, fluttering it to her mother.

Little Yíng sniffles.

He blasts off. His sneeze throws him into the cave wall. The den collapses like a pinched bubble. An avalanche buries the three spelunkers.

They laugh.

They laugh so much that they forget lunch until Mr. Wòng digs them out.

Sister Maleia

43 "I am the only person left who knows this about me. I haven't shared - not even with you, Ah-Neõi... but I wanted to for many years.

"Many years ago, the sisters in this house were rising in the morning. They did not rise for prayer, or for breakfast, not even for their duties and chores. They rose because I was calling them - screaming for them, for anyone!

"The sister who found me - the one I call my mother - was Sister Ah-Nàh. She was the oldest sister in the house, I think almost seventy-seven! She found me by following the ducks and ducklings - they piled around the mailbox, clucking up at the post... maybe trying to shut me up!

"Sister Ah-Nàh found me bundled in an old blanket... so worn it barely covered me. She told me how my little cries shook the mailbox, rang it like a drum and made me cry even more. When she lifted me out, I went silent and straight to sleep.

"The sisters raised me from when I was a newborn... all I knew was them, and I grew up wanting to be with them. I remember they tried to make ordinary clothes for me - normal dresses and skirts - but I only wore them underneath my habit! Actually... it wasn't even my habit - I borrowed it from Mother Ah-Nàh.

"But they tried so hard to help me know I didn't have to be a sister - it wasn't a must. They took me to town, tried sending me away for school, even made beautiful summer dresses for me when I was a young teenager - I had an entire closet of fashion! Each sister thought of me as her own daughter... so I had twenty-two mothers!

"We eventually sold the dresses when I came back from town. Actually, I fled back here from school because I missed my habit. I know it sounds strange – but I liked how it embraced my face. I felt like a gem in a strong velvet case – safe and cherished.

"I still feel that way... even in this tough cloth.

"But that was only a small reason why I wanted to become a sister.

"When I was seventeen, the house allowed me to take my first step – it was a silent retreat for that entire summer's end. For forty days and forty nights I said nothing. I prayed, fasted, slept, ate, worked, and stayed quiet. I only met with a priest every morning before Mass for guidance... and that was all. They wanted the silence to hone my ears, still my soul, help me wonder why I wondered. They wanted me to hear God but I heard nothing.

"Nothing until the last few days...

"I was walking in the fields while it was raining – it rained all that final week and I wouldn't stay inside anymore. I thought: *God is having it rain for so long so I can get out to it.*

"By then the rain had filled the paddies into shallow pools. I sat at the edge of a paddy and dipped my legs in the water. It reached all the way to my knees. I sat there under the clouds all afternoon – my only umbrella was my hair.

"I watched the raindrops trace my face, dangling from my hair like Christmas ornaments. My reflection in the pool was clear even though it was raining and rippling. I started shivering – I remember when my stomach growled that my whole body growled along.

"Then the rain warmed. The drops were sweet when they met my lips. I tasted sugarcane juice... I smelled rose tea dripping down my hair and throat. I saw twelve stars dressing my hair – and my face was not mine.

"The woman I saw in the water was like none I've seen. No actress, songstress, model, artwork, sunrise or sunset was as beautiful. I was made still – could even see myself off her eye's black. Just being reflected off her eye made me different... and all her statues and icons combined can't even reflect one fraction of her... her beauty – I could not only see it, but meet it. I was meeting beauty.

"I leaned low to the pool and breathed in the tea. She just looked at me, her head tilted a little and her whole face in a smile. Even though I was looking down at her, I felt she was watching over me. The warmed rain was her arms – holding me to her heart. The distant thunder was her heartbeat. She was my true mother all along...

"And I whispered to her, so close that the water stirred under my breath... I said, 'Help me be you... help me be you...' and the rain stopped. Everything around me was dry like it never rained – everything except me... I was soaked with rose tea."

MAKING FRIENDS

44 Little Yíng's fingers swing and swipe like kung-fu choreography. He picks and flicks the air – creases the unseen paper between his hands. He trains his young muscles – masters the gestures for raising life from stale scrap. He forgets the road he walks and rehearses the many styles he discovered:

"Butterfly flaps wings!" he says – complete with strikes and poses.

"Crocodile whips tail!

"Giraffe swings neck!

"Tiger draws claws!

"Elephant stomps feet!

"Penguin dodges darts!

"Flamingo steps with stealth!"

"Yíng-Yíng talks to himself!"

He stops and lifts his eyes to Big Mòu and the gang. They stare him down. He drops his hands.

"So where did you go today? Another black-out-méh?"

"Did you dream about fighting?"

Big Mòu steps forward – snatches the butterfly nesting in Little Yíng's shirt pocket. He clutches and inspects the small grey wings. The gang laughs – interrupts the crickets and toads.

"I almost thought you finally caught one-loh!" Big Mòu says. "What is this?" The creature crumples – its body crackles as it buckles. Its wings sag from his grip like amputated shark fins.

Little Yíng says nothing.

"Where did you get this?" Big Mòu dangles the warped corpse. Little Yíng sees her faint fingerprints on the body.

"I made it myself!" he yelps.

"What?"

They look at Little Yíng. Big Mòu dissects the animal – turns it inside-out, presses its body back into newspaper. He shoves the tissue into Little Yíng's hand: "Show me."

His fingers remember the paper – dance with it, curl with it. The boys watch the resurrection.

"Butterfly flaps wings!"

Big Mòu plucks the paper creature, "Where did you learn to make this-gah?"

"By myself! I found the newspaper and I practiced."

"Impossible!"

"Possible! But it took me all day!"

"Will you teach us?" the boys ask.

Little Yíng looks at them.

They do not laugh.

"But it takes all day-waw..." he says.

"We *have* all day!"

"Can we start tomorrow?"

Big Mòu watches the boys leave him behind on the dirt road. They disappear into town with chatter, questions and kung-fu moves swirling around Little Yíng.

Big Mòu turns away from the village lights, eyes down the road, reads the darkness chasing the fireflies. The butterfly in his hand tickles his wrist – lassoes his arm with a long strand of black silk. He sees it.

Big Mòu pinches the loose hair, pulls it from the paper – peels it out like entrails.

SECRET ADMIRER

45 Mr. Wòng listens as they finish vespers. Sister Maleia's lullaby rouses him with a yawn, sends shivers that flow from spine to limbs. He soaks in it.

She sees him at the back pew. He rises while she leads her daughter from the altar.

"Good night, Mr. Wòng." She bows her head.

Lumeina brushes her hand over his arm. She feels dew.

"Sister – I'm actually not leaving tonight," he says. "I want to stay..."

She stops at the doorway.

"Are you feeling all right?" she asks, looks, reaches for his brow. Her cool palm soothes his forehead. His sweat slicks her touch.

"Yes – fine... I only want to–"

"You have a fever." She takes his hand and leads him and Lumeina out of the chapel.

"I'm fine – it's just... very warm tonight-jeh."

"Shhh... wait here until I come back." She takes Lumeina and they leave him in the bath hall. The hall vanishes from his sight.

...

Her cool palm wakes him with a shudder. Mild water cradles him in the steel tub – warming steadily from his sweat. She washes the salt from his hair – holds his head like how a nest hugs an egg. She tucks a cool rag on his brow and sees him watch her.

"Thank you..." he says. She reads his lips.

"You needed a bath anyway." She smiles. He frowns.

"How did you – get me in this tub?"

She raises her bare arm and flexes. A shy muscle peaks. They smile together.

"Sister, I'm sorry – for troubling you..."

"No, no trouble at all... this is part of what we did."

"I wanted to help..." He shuts his eyes – squeegees out sweat and water.

"Even helpers need help sometimes." She dabs the droplets at his eyelids, turns to rinse the rag. He sees her coif pull away – revealing her hair. He stares up at her – the few strands of night. She swabs his neck and glances back. "What are you looking at?" she asks.

He stargazes.

"You need rest." She raises his head.

"Please forgive me, Sister... I'm sorry..."

She stares back, "It's no trouble–"

"No – not about this..." he pauses, "about taking away your family..."

"We'll talk after you recover. You need rest-loh."

"I took you away... I'm sorry."

"Shhh... shhhh..." she stills him.

She watches him fall asleep in her arms. The water darkens first in the fading candlelight – its black face pecks at Mr. Wòng, laps his bare skin.

She lifts him, but the dark clings and inhales. Its dark breath snuffs the wick and its lips whisper to her. She remembers the voice.

Mr. Wòng's body grows heavy in her arms. The water refuses to cradle – demands to be cradled. It chills into fresh sleet. Her muscles wane and her bones ice. Her fingers anchor onto his hair and flesh – her nails drill for life.

The water darkens into abyss – into absence. Icicles sting her grip, their shattering bodies squeal for her. She hears their sirens call up from the deep – calls of hunger and feeding.

Her hands bite into Mr. Wòng. Warmth spills from him and melts through her. He drips into the dark. Other hands press around her – clench her as much as she clenches him. Her muscles buckle with her bones and she falls over

the chasm's rim – his body trawls her along. The hungry
breathe them in.

    They fall together.

VENENUM

46 Lumeina finds the man and woman – still singing their song, still dancing their days away. She watches them hold each other – like sky holding clouds, like night holding starlight. They gaze at each other – through and into each other with the peace of the interior gaze.

Their flesh is clean and young – always ripe and never riper. They sweat and weep honey for one another's thirst. His body is all of him – not a drop of blood is against him. Her body is all of her – not a pulse is defiant. His body is his face – her body is hers, and together they are Love's. Together they wander the gift.

The great trees offer their best sweets – their trunks and arms curtsy and bow their ornaments before the man and woman. The couple tastes all and all tastes good.

They wander past a tree with two high branches and a proud trunk. Its sap drools down its body and penetrates the earth. The man gazes up the tree and reads its leaves fanning the breeze. The sun dusts the sifting leaves – lets him see into the tree's lush crown. A brother sleeps within the hanging garden – tucked upon a bed of wood.

Smoke rises up to the brother. The man watches the wind darken. The dark wind unsheathes its talons, strips the tree naked, scourges its tender bark, gnaws its core for thick sap. Leaves fall to the ground like singed skin.

The brother is taken from his bed and pinned to the tree's spine. The wind claws his dripping face with a kiss. The wind sears his breaths with cinder. The wind wrings his flesh for sweat – wrings for blood and water.

The man watches the wind pluck and juice the brother. The tree's proud trunk sags with sap even thicker – even richer. Its roots flow as rivers red with warmth. The earth drinks.

The wind casts off the brother – swift gusts consume his body. The tree returns to new life.

The dark wind falls from the tree onto the man, surrounds him and threatens. It pecks his ears and prods his song.

He stops singing.

He steps aside.

The smoke proceeds to his bride, it softens and runs through the woman's hair. It wraps her with whispers – asks her to stare, to doubt and to want. She peers into the new leaves and the new fruits. She reaches for their great height and the wind lowers the branches – presses the tree's arms to her feet.

The wind woos her with its old song and old caresses.

The tree bleeds white.

The woman tastes the tree's unripe seed. Lonesomeness fills her appetite. The seed's bitter blood stains her black. She shares with the man and he watches the black blood. He remembers the dark wind – threatening... threatening.

He takes.

Doubt feeds the man's stomach with hunger – the woman's womb with sorrow. The dark wind laughs at the man and woman.

The man's body pulses against his will. The woman's body bleeds against her.

The dark wind rains leeches onto the man and woman. The black worms lather their naked bodies in black sputum. The long thin maggots swell and plump as they burrow the couple's stale flesh – lacing the woman's heart with chains and the man's strength with tyranny. The smoke blackens into squid ink and climbs into their mouths – chews through their teeth and claws down their throats. It mines them and plants mines deep in their bones.

Black rain stains the gift. All around the man and woman, flowers burn brown, leaves pepper the air with their ashes, waters drown their fish, and lands starve their animals. The song ends and wailing begins.

The man and woman do not hold each other. His sweat burns her flesh and her touch accuses his skin – like lightning blistering clouds and piercing sky. He stares at her body and will not see her face. She hides from his stare because of his face. She hides under dead leaves and he hides with her.

The sun searches for them – longs for the man and woman. The light walks and finds the man and woman hidden beneath black festers and tinder. They look away. The sun's gaze shames their flesh. Their bodies lose their luster.

The woman looks to the man and weeps in the light. The man raises his finger to the light and points another to the woman. His finger draws her tears.

The woman finds a leech suckling her. She sheds the plump worm and flings it to her heel. She points down to the dark scar writhing in dust beside her – too fattened to flee.

INFESTATION MANIFESTATION

47 The scar fattens to the edges of Lumeina's sight – blackens the view within her like a photograph charring into shadow. She wakes into darkness and silence. Her hands and feet search the coarse sheets only to find more sheets. The frays are cool and untouched except by her. She smells for her mother, but breathes only aged aromas. Her breaths are alone.

Lumeina toes the grooves in the floor – some familiar and some strange. The unknown cracks are fine, thin – sprawling the concrete like wet hair. She stoops to the new lines and reads their direction, follows them to a wall, up the wall and all about the hallway.

The cracks cluster and furrow into warped faces – some glare at her, some grin at her, wince at her, but all watch her. Their eyes stalk her as she follows their hairs.

The hallway splinters into deep dark fissures all around Lumeina – swallowing her in a throat coiled with veins. The cracks reach far into the walls and floors – farther than the walls and floors are thick, deeper than bottomless pits.

Lumeina crawls the halls – the serrated fractures nip her fingers, knees and feet. The strangers overwhelm the familiar. She feels no sun where an open window welcomes dawn. She rises to the ledge and tastes for morning – listens for day, but an absence deafens her and numbs her tongue.

She remembers licking unripe persimmon.

The flavor smothers her tongue in chalk.

Lumeina coughs into the wall. Dust puffs from the cracks like black snow, clings to her hair and nose. Charcoal syrup wets her lips and taints her spit. The tar splatters to the floor and each droplet springs forth eight legs. The long legs grope for her.

She remembers the spider's bed – the delicate thread against her fingertip.

The threads grow barbs. They latch onto her hair, gown, limbs and skin – then reel her down to the crumbling floor. The wires fasten her cheek to the concrete. The floor wrinkles around her face and licks. The strange faces hem her in and writhe up against her – kissing and grasping.

Lumeina strains to push away. She pulls into a ball, slaps and kicks, but the floor buries her hands and clamps her knees in its crust. She breathes – chokes on the black syrup. The long legs stitch her mouth shut and stuff her ears with her own hair.

...

Little Yíng hears mortar and pestle – muffled and steady grinding. He pushes into the house and waits for his eyes.

He waits but the dark is too dark.

He calls out for Lumeina and her mother. He hears only himself. He enters and searches.

The hallway is gritty under his feet. He rubs the sand from his sole and touches the floor. He looks down and the dark is deep and solid. He cannot see his feet, his hands or body. Little Yíng turns to find the door but black stares back.

He blinks and opens his eyes. He opens his eyes but they are already open. He cannot tell.

"Ah-Fei? Ah-Luu?" he calls.

Little Yíng searches the floor for her guide grooves. His fingers and toes brush and dig into the sand. He pats the walls and they feel like the floor. He follows the wall – finds blackened windows and smacks the glass. He scratches the glass and it bites at his nails.

Little Yíng stumbles and trips over a boulder – his heels kick into moss and he falls backward over the rock. He catches a handful of lichen and leaps off Lumeina. He releases her hair. He huddles close and finds her – says her name over and over.

Tears and snot muddle his cries. He touches for his friend and finds a thick band of stone binding her small body – constricting her in its cage. Little Yíng beats his fists onto the stone band, grips it and twists. He traces the fat rope wrapping Fei from neck to ankles. It emerges from the floor and sinks into it again.

He pries at the statue and it hisses. Little Yíng stops – then pries again. He snatches a broken floor tile and stabs the thing's hide. The tile shatters and disappears into the creature.

"Luu!" he shouts – stumbles for someone to help, "Sister Maleia! Mr. Wòng! Ah-Fei!"

He remembers her father.

Slivers of light slice through the dark.

Little Yíng recognizes the constellation. He keeps shouting for Ah-Bàh and watches the lit wings swim the black sea. The butterfly cuts past kelp and weed, trap and snare, hook and line, fang and tentacle. It perches on Little Yíng's right arm and becomes his lantern.

His hands are red and the serpent is black. Lumeina sleeps in the snake's embrace – her own hair strapping her to the floor. The serpent conceals its fangs inside her heels – its skin suppurates under the lantern.

Little Yíng strikes the snake's center. His elbow smashes the black stone in two, in three, into pieces like a charcoal statue. It hisses into dust. The dark seeps into the cracks and sucks away its cremains.

Day breaks through the window without splintering the glass.

The butterfly hops upon Lumeina's hair and rests with her. Little Yíng does the same.

SECRET DESIRER

48 The boys find Big Mòu home alone. They stand in the doorway of the small house.

"When is he coming back-waw?"

"I don't even know where he went-ah!" Big Mòu says.

"He promised to teach us origami today!"

"He promised-lah!"

Big Mòu shushes them – holds up the crinkled butterfly. They stare at the paper and watch him gut the insect. The lone strand is long, black and supple. He says nothing and listens.

"That's only your mom's hair!"

"None of our moms have hair like that!"

"I've never seen hair that long!"

They watch the noon sun skim along the strand. They reach for the relic.

"Does it smell good-mah?"

"Wah! So soft-ah!"

They all pluck the violin string – fondling its tips and rubbing its luster.

"Yíng-Yíng is hiding someone from us," Big Mòu says. Their eyes follow the strand as he coils it around his thumb.

"Who?"

"Who!"

"A movie star!"

"A chick!"

Big Mòu pushes past them and they follow him to the street, out of town, onto the pocked road.

Bathing in Abyss

49 Lumeina's face is against Little Yíng's head. She presses close, dips her nose into his nape. She breathes, tastes that it is not a dream.

Little Yíng springs to his shins and sits up. He helps her and holds her in his sigh, "You're awake-lah..."

Rashes, cuts and scrapes tint her pink and red. "Fei... are you hurt-mah?" He touches the streaks across her cheek. The sweat on his fingertips tingles her wounds. She smiles and shakes her head. He tingles as her voice flows from her fingertips: *I don't know what happened...*

She sniffles.

You're bleeding!

Little Yíng pulls his hand away, "It's nothing-lah – it's dry-lah. Where's your mother-néh?"

Fei climbs to her feet, then ducks. She spreads her arms out and moves slow, trembling. Her feet sense the floor's cracks. She stomps them, grinds her heels into them, stomps and stomps until Little Yíng calms her, "They're gone... not here anymore-lah – I saw them leave..."

She grips the knotted cord at her waist and clutches the loops like a pearl necklace. She wonders a mystery and finds the grooves along the floor. They follow the guide lines throughout the house until the odor of Mother spills into her nose.

She stops.

She tears into the bath hall. She finds the steel tub battered into a corner and two breaths twitching from within. Fei dips her arms into the tub and swings her hands through emptiness. She reaches in further than the tub is deep.

Little Yíng peers into the tub and remembers the blank black stare. He pulls his friend away from the hole, "There's nothing in there-gah!"

Fei struggles. She inhales rose tea.

Little Yíng finds a chip of floor tile, drops it into the tub. They wait for an answer.

Luu snatches a tin pail and slams it into the pit's gaping jaw. They lean their ears to the abyss.

Moments pass.

They only hear one another waiting.

"How's this happening-gah?" Little Yíng says.

Fei reaches into the black, writes for her mother in the dark air – her fingers scream into the absence.

He watches her.

"Sister Maleia?" he shouts down. The depths swallow his voice and eat his echo. He tries again – but only whispers.

Luu climbs over the rim and jumps into the tub. Little Yíng screams and leaps in after her.

The tub bulges, explodes like a sick watermelon – it spews out Lumeina, her mother, Little Yíng and Mr. Wòng like four stout seeds. The steel rind twists away in a clang – shrieks like a gong. They sprawl out on the floor.

The adults are limp and sipping for air – the children are clasped together like two hands pleading in prayer.

SONG OF SONGS

50 Little Yíng carries a can of warm water to Lumeina. He holds still as she dips a cloth, soaks, wrings, wipes Mr. Wòng's face. She places a hand over his heart and listens to it wrestle.

She scoots to her mother asleep nearby on a neat bed of rags. She lays her ear on her mother's breast. Her face and skull reverberate with Mother's beat. She remembers dreams in dark warm waters. She writes on her mother's belly with slow strokes – her fingerprints smudge the habit.

Little Yíng waves a sheet of cardboard – rolling the humid air onto their soggy bodies. He watches Fei's hair cling to the wind and rise like a bloom. A dark face appears in her curtain of hair – staring at him. He recognizes the fangs. He stops fanning.

The strands fall lank and drape her in a hood and mantle. Little Yíng nears his friend as she waters her mother's body with teardrops. He kneels on the other side of her mother and takes her hands. They sit on their shins – huddle over her mother and breathe together.

"I'm staying – I'm not leaving-lah," he says.

She grips him tighter.

She lets go and finds Mother's yellowed cord of knots. They thumb the beads together over her mother's heart and navel. Luu helps him know what to chant. He sings for both of them:

AVE MARÍA...
GRÁTIA PLENA, DÓMINUS TECUM...
BENEDÍCTA TU IN MULIÉRIBUS ET BENEDÍCTUS FRUCTUS
VENTRIS TUI.
IESUS...

The song reaches out – melts into the air held between their touch, entwines them together. Their foreheads rest against one another:

SANCTA MARÍA MATER DEI...
ORA PRO NOBIS PECCATÓRIBUS,
NUNC ET IN HORA MORTIS NOSTRÆ...

Their sweat blends, their wounded hands weld, their blood blends into one.

AMEN...

They feel nothing else.

THE GIRL

51 "Yíng-Yíng!"
Shouting whacks their ears.
"Yíng-Yíng! We know you're in there-gah!"
"You lied to us-ah!"
"Come out-ah!"

The ruckus whacks their prayers. Little Yíng shuts up and opens his eyes. Fei prays on – her bandages moist with both their tears and sweat, her lips near enough to taste him. He turns his ears from her breaths and listens to rough footsteps in the garden. He hears boy hands snap twigs and rip fruits.

The sticks peck the house and the fruits smear its face.

Little Yíng squeezes Luu before leaving her. He rushes outside. She asks for help.

Before turning down the main hallway, Little Yíng notices the chapel. He stops at the doorway and mimics Fei: kneels flat to the floor, then taps his mind, heart and strength with his right hand ✚. He looks to the mangled man dangling from the wall and sighs:

pater noster...
qui es in cælis. sanctificétur nomen tuum.
advéniat regnum tuum. fiat volúntas tua...
sicut in cælo et in terra...
panem nostrum quotidiánum da nobis hódie.
et dimítte nobis débita nostra.
sicut et nos dimíttimus debitóribus nostris:
et ne nos indúcas in tentatiónem.
sed líbera nos a malo...

"Don't make us drag you out-ah!"
"We're not afraid-gah!"

Little Yíng rises and peers around the corner. Down the hall, the boys loiter on the doorsteps. The evening sun hides his silhouette in the shaded house. He walks in quiet and meets them. They are loud.

"Yíng-Yíng! Thought you could hide from us-méh?"

"What are you doing here-ah?"

"What is this place-ah?"

They poke him with branches and haul him down the steps. He covers his face. Big Mòu draws the dark strand from its spool around his thumb, dangles it over Little Yíng's face.

He grins when Little Yíng uncovers.

"Familiar-mah?" Big Mòu says.

"Your mom?" Little Yíng says – stands straight. They shove him into Big Mòu.

"Why does everyone think that!" Big Mòu shakes Little Yíng, "Who is she? Tell me now!"

"You better tell Dài Mòu everything!"

"Everything! You liar!"

Little Yíng pushes away and knocks into the boys behind him. They all stumble.

"Is she inside? You think she belongs to you-méh? There aren't enough girls in this country for wimps!" Big Mòu wrenches the smaller boy to the ground but he does not lower. Little Yíng springs back up and glares.

"Who is she!" Big Mòu tosses the strand and snatches his hair.

Little Yíng winces but snares Big Mòu's throat – pinches his fingertips around the crunchy pipe. He whispers into Big Mòu's face, "She is a secret."

Big Mòu shoots snot from his nostrils. Green mud and morsels smack Little Yíng's face. He trips aside and the boys clamp him to the ground. "Wrong-lah Yíng-Yíng! She's mine-gah! Now you're coming back with us!"

"I can't! Never!"

"Méh? You're living with her-àh? She's mine-gah!" He kicks dirt onto Little Yíng. "Mom and Dad will beat you to death!"

"They're not my parents!" He swings a rock into the boys' shins – chops them down and draws sap. They scrunch into whimpering armadillos.

Big Mòu stomps on them, "Get up! All of you!"

Little Yíng stands while the boys ball up behind Big Mòu.

"Get out of here-ah! Jàu-ah!" Little Yíng shouts. He points to the fields.

"Good you're not coming back! No one likes you anyway – that's why your parents ran and left you with us!"

"Shut up Mòu-Mòu!"

"They buried you and ran! We found you naked in the basement! You came with the house!"

Little Yíng raises and aims the rock, but they all fall still and silent. They stare past him. He follows their sights – finds Lumeina standing in the doorway.

"Fei..." Little Yíng gasps. Her bandages droop like soggy tissues, her hair is grimy in the setting sun and her gown is a kiwi-skin quilt.

"What a funny face..."

"She looks like she smells..."

"Someone shitted on her..."

"Toilet paper face..."

"*She's your girlfriend?*"

"Her face is unfinished!"

"Unfinished face!"

"Ahh! Unfinished face! Jàu-ah!"

"Jàu-ah!"

And they run and laugh and leave.

Luu smiles and hurries to her friend. She feels the sun pull away from the sky and from their bodies. She feels nightfall embrace them.

PALISADES

52 His fingers are a vise on the steel lid. The alloy slides through green bones. Marrow slicks the blade. Little Yíng watches where he cuts and where he holds the can's lid. He stops every few strokes and adjusts his grip – fluffs the cushion of air between hand and razor.

Around him are granite fragments – etched and polished with dates of birth and dates of death. Yíng clears a narrow path through the rubble. A pile of bamboo stakes rest behind him. From there, a palisade processes back to where construction began – the javelins coil the land like a sleeping eel skeleton. Its ribs stand guard against the sea of weeds – steady in the waves like urchin spikes and angler fangs. The pineapple swordsmen hide behind the reef, ready for war.

Little Yíng takes fresh bamboo and sharpens its ends into spear points. The shavings coil at his feet like overgrown toenails. A trail of clipped toenails loops the grounds like a foamy moat – complete with crocodile jaws. Little Yíng feels every stroke and cut tingle through the tooth's vein.

...

Lumeina rests Mother's head on her lap, cups her hands over her heart. She sits with her sleeping mother, counts her pulse, feels her bloodstreams and breaths. She counts with the worn rosary woven between her hands.

Mr. Wòng dreams nearby in the bedroom with origami animals huddling his sides – moving with his breathing. A giraffe leans on his damp brow.

...

Little Yíng stakes the ground with another lance. His sweat stains the soil with dark moles. He deepens the bite but the ground resists. The tooth finds a filling.

Little Yíng crouches close and digs into the gum. The bamboo tooth gnaws into a nest of turtle eggs. He drops the stake. He stares at the clutch.

The silver eggs share an umbilical cord linking one to the next. Little Yíng pulls the steel chain out and dust crumbles away. He thumbs the cold pearls – hears Lumeina. His lips move. He follows the links to a medal and scrapes clay off its face. He finds new shapes: a dozen stars and two hearts – one crowned with thorns and the other pierced with a sword.

Both bleed fire together.

He turns the medal over and finds a woman looking back at him – waiting to hold him. He stops to gaze. She holds him and leads him to a mangled man affixed to sticks. Grit clings to his body like open wounds.

Little Yíng remembers him – a bigger him.

He wraps the loop around his fist and runs to the house.

...

She hears his steps and his pace, listens to him pump water – a new sound rattles with him. She follows the rattle through the house until he finds her. His swift breaths do not tire.

Little Yíng kneels beside Lumeina. He touches her hands, lifts the frayed cord from her fingers and nestles the heavy seeds into her palms. She does not move.

"Luu..." he nudges.

Her sweat steams the stainless steel pearls. He watches fog wrap the gleaming beads. Lumeina feels the eggs incubate in her grasp.

"I just found it-guh – outside..."

She brings the nest to her lips. The iron is familiar to her nose and tongue. She smiles and lays the bouquet upon her mother's breast.

Her fingers cradle the crucifix and read the prayer crowning the rose tea lady:

SHADOW PUPPETS

53 Blue moonlight frames the window with ice – stains the room and all things within. Luu and Little Yíng sit below the sill. She leans on his shoulder, asleep while he watches the walls – listens to their breaths. The chain of silver eggs clinks in his fingers like a wind chime – dangles like strung drops of sea.

The moon moves. Shadows of trees sprout into view – their branches spread onto the walls like coral fingers. The hands tremble and shiver. The silhouettes grasp the wall and run like black ink. Little Yíng watches them finger-paint.

They gesture.

Their bodies mold into puppets, and the puppets amass into shoals of fins and tails. Reefs bloom from the dark branches and glitter with glowing colors. Baby sea turtles paddle through the waters like swimming stones. Pink fish puff into sea roses. Kelp clumps sway like summer willows.

"Fei... Ah-Fei..." Little Yíng whispers for her. He turns his face into her hair and nuzzles. Her hair is sweet and her sweat smells like ripe rain.

The creatures gather around her mother and Mr. Wòng asleep nearby on the seafloor. Others gather close to him and Lumeina. Bubbles dribble from their mouths while they stare at the sleeping.

They stare for a long time.

Little Yíng stares back. Their bodies shed scales and flesh – dust the seabed with snow. Sea anemones shrivel into black viscera. Sea stars crumble into scabs. Sea urchins snare others in their needles. Seahorses tumble headless into the dark. The blued walls fill with fish skeletons, whale skulls, empty shells, eel teeth, medusa jellies and octopus ink. The floating graveyard swims around them – leaps from wall to wall and floor to ceiling.

Her mother and Mr. Wòng are gone under the dead seabed. Worms emerge from the floor to feed. Little Yíng draws in his feet and shields Fei. The black bones tap on her sleeping body. Empty eye sockets lust for Luu. They tempt him to lust too. They undo her seams and undress her.

Little Yíng whacks the skeletons off her. He mends her gown. The bones scatter. They collect into piles and recombine into claws.

They return even darker, even more numerous.

They wait.

The hands claw the walls – the ocean around him shatters into shards. The fingers scrape until their bones grind down to fists. Ruckus buffets the room – the noise of lightning pealing through clouds but never clapping.

He shouts at the shadows, "Quiet! Quiet-lah! I'm not afraid-gah!"

The bony hands stretch and crack their knuckles. They reach around the two children and flick Little Yíng's face – bruise his eyes, blister his cheeks and slap him silent. He holds onto Luu and does not loosen.

The hands pry his eyelids and put on a puppet show. He recognizes the mangled man drooping from the dark cross – his own black blood smothering him. Lampreys nip his sores and urchins grate his skull. The man's face falls off and smacks the floor like a sweat rag. Little Yíng watches a new face fester into place – a familiar nose, familiar eyes, familiar lips and cheeks.

Little Yíng sees himself, his own black blood smothers himself. The puppeteers skin his puppet and pierce his doll with needles. They staple his shadow to the wood and let them rot together.

Little Yíng clings to Lumeina and tears his eyelids from their grip.

"I don't care what you do! You can't have her!" Little Yíng opens the loop of steel beads and crowns Fei with the wreath. The pearls fall to her collar and shoulders – the medal rests on her heart and the crucifix floats over her lung.

Little Yíng wraps Fei in himself, and her hair enwraps them. He whispers with the roses and routs the banshees.

STIGMATESS

54 Lumeina wakes from between her mother and Mr. Wòng. Their warm bodies cling to her bare arms. The rosary clings to her chest. She reaches for it, fondles the medal and finds the lady with open arms.

She presses her lips to Mother's palm and rubs her face into it – moves her mouth and speaks through touch: *Wake soon-lah, Ah-Máh... stop sleeping-lah...*

Her lips meet the lips of a wound. Her tongue peeks out and taps the hollow – tastes the marrow. She smells it, then slides Mother's hand to her cheek. The hole in her hand brands Daughter's face with a streak.

Lumeina puts her finger into the wound. She finds knucklebones and tendons, navigates the cavern to the other side.

Ah-Máh?

Daughter crawls to Mother's feet: her fingers creep from her knee to her ankle, rounds her heel, and into the hole. The passageway guides her fingertip through the sole.

Lumeina checks.

Both feet match both hands – Mother's wounds match the man's.

UNFINISHED FACE

55 Lumeina sits under the altar in the chapel. She
scrolls through the aged pages – traces her mother's
fingerprints. The hands guide Lumeina through crowds and
kingdoms, through thousands and millions until she finds
the man and the doubter.

She hears Mother read to her.

She listens.

Coughs interrupt her. She listens for him but finds only
his coughs – outside. She listens to dry breath sting its way
up a dry throat into dry cheeks. She kisses Mother's
handprints, kisses the page before leaving the chapel.

The whine of the well pump fills the quiet house.

...

Lumeina follows the rustle of bamboo leaves and
splitting shoots. Her feet follow the trail of overgrown
toenail clippings. The morning sun tingles her skin with
little massages – the sky dusts her hair and clothes. She grips
the cans of water – catches leaked droplets with her toes.

She catches the scent of Little Yíng and bleeding
bamboo. She stops when a pile of stakes poke her approach.
Her shadow shades him from the day.

"Fei!" He turns to her and takes the cans. She smiles,
writes on his shoulder with her cold fingers: *You sound thirsty.*

He tastes the water, sets down his empty can and takes
her hand. He leads her to shade.

...

Luu and Little Yíng's legs dip into the mud paddy like chopsticks in black sesame pudding. They sit at the paddy's edge, drink the cool pudding – sip the coolness through their feet and up their thin shins.

Fei touches her friend's hand. His vein squirms from her fingertip. He opens his palm to her: *What were you doing out here – making what?*

"A fence... to protect you."

But I have the pineapples. I smell them – they're still on guard.

Little Yíng sees the guerillas along the palisade.

See their swords? Lots of them...

Little Yíng listens. He looks at the rustling blades, searches across the smooth dark paddy. He sees the shadows of tall grey clouds. A pineapple plant loses its head. Fei perks – touches again: *Footsteps – many.*

The boys walk the field – split a pineapple and share the spoils. Their brisk feet smack dust like marching boots. Little Yíng grits his teeth.

He helps Lumeina up. The mud glues their soles to the ground. Their legs are chocolate covered cookie sticks.

"Wey! You two going somewhere?"

"Leave us alone..." Little Yíng says. Lumeina grips his arm with both hands. She turns her head away from the angry boys.

"We only wanted to visit *Mei-Yeen-Meen*. Did God finish her face yet?" Big Mòu says.

"Stop calling her that!"

Luu buries her bandaged face into her friend's back. He feels the peanut shells over her eyes press hard against him. She feels his muscles swell with blood, his skin spew sweat.

The four boys spread out – surround the two.

Hands snag her arms. They sting her with pinches. They nip her and twist her from Little Yíng. He swings at them but the others snatch him. Lumeina opens her mouth, breathes and breathes to scream nothing but silence. Little Yíng watches from his knees, "Don't touch her!"

Big Mòu pushes Fei to the dirt, pins her back against the path. He feels her swell under him. He swells too.

"Leave Luu alone!"

"Throw Yíng-Yíng in the mud!" They drag Little Yíng to the paddy and plunge him into the black lava. Big Mòu waits for help to hold her down. They take turns calling her *Mei-Yeen-Meen! Mei-Yeen-Meen! Mei-Yeen-Meen!*

Lumeina trembles beneath them. Her belly balloons and falls like skin on a war-drum. The steel pearls tumble along her chest like a rockslide. The boys stare at the tinkling clutch and watch her sweat rust.

Big Mòu turns to the twin red blotches bulging from her blindfolds. He peels the tight bands from her eyes. He claws her – pares off yards and yards like a mad hairdresser. The stains grow fiercer with every thinning layer.

Stripped bandages surround the boys in a mess of glaring bloodshot eyes. Her black hair hides the eyes in caverns. Her red sweat crawls along her flesh, gown, and bandages – it paints itself into their portraits.

The boys recognize themselves in the inkblots. They stop calling her *Mei-Yeen-Meen.*

Wind tosses up the bleeding tentacles – binding the boys in a swarm. The suckers spit hot ink into Big Mòu's face. The boys scream and gargle mouthfuls of dark chocolate.

Yíng charges at them. He scoops more mud off his body, aims and slings – all in rapid-fire. Mòu-Mòu trips and scurries from Fei. He wipes his eyes but the tar clings – smears under his eyelids.

Yíng rushes to Mòu-Mòu and crouches low to his face. He aims – breakfast gas sputters from deep within his tunnels. The butt burp bubbles through his pants and spurts mud onto Mòu-Mòu's face.

Mòu-Mòu shrieks into the ground. The boys fall quiet and whimper off. Mòu-Mòu trails far behind before wading into the weeds.

Quick breaths and shivers catch Yíng's ears. He huddles close to Fei and lifts her head. Her face is wrinkled with a quivering smile – laughing in giddy silence. Her eyelids leak sour honey – drip like mashed pomegranates.

Yíng watches her eyes.

She touches her friend's muddy body and draws characters – tattoos him through the muck: *Eeeeeeh! Your fart smells like peanut butter!*

LIGHT FROM LIGHT

56 Rain dilutes her pomegranate juice. The mud on their bodies trickles into chocolate milk. Yíng leans over Lumeina's eyes – becomes her umbrella – but she reaches out and catches fresh drops in her mouth. She catches the rain with her whole body, opens herself to the falling ocean.

He watches her chase the rain, watches her hair whip and cling as she leaps and hops. The earth sprays her legs and daubs her knees. The rain drags her rags and licks her stains clean.

Luu finds Yíng and fishes him from the puddles. She warms the raindrops around them – warms him in her embrace. Her fingers read his spine and ribs – kneading the bones of his back.

"Ah-Fei... we should go inside-lah..."

Luu shakes her head and returns to the sky. She listens to the rain pet her face, drip through her hair – drip through his. He looks up with her and blinks off the drops. He stops blinking and sees the sky glisten. Puddles pool in the gaps between their bodies.

The clouds shatter like giant dishes. Broken crumbs pepper down like pellets. Yíng snatches Luu and they flee from the sky's sight – flee straight into the mud paddy.

The black batter sucks them in and tucks itself everywhere. Fei feels the mud hug her body in a snug glove. Fog rises from the warm muck and hides her from Yíng. He finds her toes in the cookie dough.

She kicks.

He follows her body to her face and finds her giggling again.

That tickles! You're tickling me!

Her kicking flings pudding at him. He laughs – helps Fei to her feet, but the mud weighs her down. She topples onto him and they flop. They try again and he tumbles into her.

They try and try – plop and plop, each stumbling after lifting up the other. They laugh and laugh with the thunder. They surrender to the rain, admire the veins warming the storm's grey bosom.

...

Yíng finally pulls Fei from the paddy. Their arms are slick. They grip each other's clothes. On land again, the rain drowns them with more. Thick drops etch through their mud coats. Yíng throws off his shirt and wipes down his pants. He rinses the shirt in the downpour and scrubs Lumeina's hair with it.

Her hair lightens as he washes her. She stands still but tiptoes to touch the sky – clasps for it with her fingertips, pinches the clouds like chopsticks. Yíng turns away and rinses the rag again.

The sky touches her.

It clasps her with its fingers.

It pinches her pink.

Her hair – every strand stands rigid like a molten white needle. The tips of her hair are crumbs of sun. Her flesh blinds Yíng and singes his hair. Her mud crackles into crystals. Her gown flares off into yellow flakes and petals – but her body does not burn. She is not consumed. Her veins channel the lightning like wires in a lit bulb. Her lips, ears, nose, navel and holes fill with glow – and the scabs over her eyes incinerate into fresh flesh.

Yíng gazes at sunrise and sunset. The crown of needles melts black and lank, and Lumeina sits on a fresh bed of glass. Steam lays her down on its cushion – blankets her. Her flesh tosses incense.

Yíng does not move until the rain falls again. It boils away on her glass bed and hushes off her skin. He approaches

– reaches. She is merely warm to his touch. Gems adorn her shoulders, nape, collar and chest. The white pearls fade to yellow, to orange, then red before settling into silver again. The links between the eggs are new veins. The medal is tucked in Lumeina's breast. The crucifix is pierced to her side – fused to her rib.

Yíng traces the steel moles. They are firm under his fingers. The rag is clean – dry in his hands. He veils her body. He lifts her in his arms and carries her home.

HEMOGRAPHESS

57 Yíng fills a gown with Lumeina – fills it with life. Her clean body warms the fibers. Yíng rests her beside her mother. He does not notice Mr. Wòng – gone and missing. He kneels at her side until his joints set and his bones bond. He eats and drinks nothing and his stomach whispers with him. He grips the knots. He kisses the beads melded into Luu.

After he kisses the lady on the medal, he rises and walks through the dark halls. His stiffened body snaps with each step. At the chapel, he bows and enters. He finds the skeleton of wire and wood veiled behind curtains of dripping leaks. The floor is a rippling mirror.

He crosses the puddles and stands beneath the crude crucifix. Water runs down the man, trickles from his gored feet onto Yíng's head. He looks up, watches the water flow over corrosion and navigate lacerations. He looks. He beholds.

He hears a song.

Yíng hurries to the kitchen, returns with armfuls of empty jars and cans. He sets them under the leaks, traps the invaders and goes for more containers. He does not stop until he outfits the chapel with an organ. It whistles while he works. He listens to the storm play. It plays for days.

...

Yíng holds Lumeina's hair in his lap – its long weight floats like a ghost. He tunes the Chinese zither as best he can with loops of twine – careful not to pluck any strings. The warm bundle runs like a black breeze in his arms. It bathes him.

A red halo lacquers around Fei's head – widening with every drop from her eyes. Her tears and blood blend into orange ova with crimson pips. The ikura roll from the corners of her eyes, turn the curves of her earlobes, hang like earrings.

The organ whistles while she weeps.

Ying waits for the next ruby to drop. It disappears into the cloth – adds to her corona. He cradles Lumeina's head and replaces the damp pillow with a new. He folds the stain and sets it on a pile of others. He blows out the candle, lies beside and stares down the dark.

The night stares right back.

The Interior Gaze

58 The butterfly leans on Lumeina's breath. Its feet cling to her cheek – its tongue anoints the lips of her eyes. The butterfly sips her bitter nectar until she drips sweet.

Luu sniffs the wet morning. She follows the butterfly's steps, her breaths ricochet off its wings. She waits for it to finish – she waits and the rain plays for her. The butterfly grooms her eyelashes. Luu steadies her mute giggles.

The silk feet lift from her face – the wings unveil her to the day.

She rubs the tickles from her eyes. Syrup flavors her fingers. Soft skin kisses her touch. She seeks her bandages and scabs but finds only satin.

She opens her eyes and they open. She stares at the light and it stares back. She blinks – takes a bite – and the day does not flee.

The butterfly sashays overhead. Fei watches the stars on its black wings. She follows them as they shoot to her side. The meteor shower lands in a patch of short hair.

She gasps.

Luu leans up – gazes at Yíng. She hears him and sees him. She does not blink as she watches her hand brush his ear – his ear bending against her fingertips, his hair parting between her knuckles, his lips tasting her syrup.

She watches him wake.

Her eyes swallow him.

He drowns into her.

Neither speaks but sees. He sees himself on the sheen of her black iris – sees himself inside her. She sees herself on the shine of his eyes – warm within him. They gaze and touch and watch one another gaze.

He rises and they wrap each other. "Fei..." he whispers her into ear – tastes the blossom. He listens to her fingertips vibrate into him:

Yíng...

"I missed you so much... are you hurt-mah? Hungry-mah? Are you thirsty–" Luu puts her fingers to his lips. He quiets. She runs her fingers along his back – taps his ribs like piano keys:

What is that song?

They listen together.

The rain is singing...

She listens and follows the music – first with her ears, then with her feet. He and she step and sway their way through the halls. Her eyes taste the moist grey day with glee.

She finds the concert.

They bow and enter the chapel. The jars chirp and the cans whistle. The room echoes – their breaths and steps follow. They dance in the dripping song – they catch it in her hair, catch it on his shoulders, catch it on their soles.

Luu lifts her lips to the drops. She watches the rain miss her mouth and splash Yíng. They laugh and press together. Her steel scars rasp between them – lodged against his chest and against her bones.

Did my mother wake? I want her to hear this...

Yíng's next step spills a full jar.

The water stretches out and smothers the song.

Smothered.

I want to see her... I want her to see my eyes. Ah-Bàh finished! And where's Mr. Wòng?

Yíng holds Lumeina, keeps her cheek close to his. She feels his warmth abandon him – abandon them. They stop moving.

"I don't know where Mr. Wòng is... he's been gone–"

Yíng – where's my mom?

His body is cold and shivering.

"She started to smell..." he says. His jaws jitter.

But I don't smell her...

"She smelled bad... I tried to wash her but she–"

My mom smells good. Where is she? I can't smell her.

Yíng says nothing. His tears chill Fei's shoulder and abrade her back. Her fingers gnaw his spine:

Yíng! Where is she? Tell me!

He opens to her.

She sees.

She sees her flesh sunken into her bones – sees her flesh curled away, her body too white for life and too still for sleep.

Luu pushes away from Yíng. She falls onto a crowd of jars and thrashes them into shards. She cries into the puddles and they ripple with her weeping.

"Fei... Fei!" Yíng swoops to her. She crawls the aisle and casts the cans into the pews, into the walls and windows. She smacks the floor like a stranded mermaid. She smears the rain with red – paints a face into the water. The puddles blush warm and the face in the water is not hers.

Lumeina calms – gazes into the sheen.

The woman in the water sighs. Tea fogs the cool air. Her breath fluffs the raindrops into mist – cuddles Lumeina in a robe of cirrus.

Luu dips her fingers into the water, then her hands. Her arms reach full into the puddle and meet the woman.

Her face is soft with sunshine. Her lips remind Lumeina of ripe strawberry wombs. She smiles as Lumeina reads her face with eyes and hands.

PALACE AIDES

59 Yíng watches Fei peer into the floor, dip into it – disappear into it. He sees only her legs and waist left on land. He approaches on his knees.

The haze thickens around Fei – blotches Yíng out. He watches her vanish in the cloud. He stops and listens.

Lumeina soaks in the well – bathes in her gaze. The woman writes on Lumeina's cheek with a caress. Lumeina's tears fall into the woman's eyes.

The woman begins to feel wet in her arms – feels like a damp floor.

Luu scribbles onto the concrete – her fingernails splinter against the grain: *Don't leave me... not you too...*

Fei claws the floor, grasps the cold with her body.

...

Yíng listens to her sniffles in the fog.

He hears the ducks squeal in the rain – all of them squealing like piglets.

Then muzzled one by one.

The ducks disappear.

Yíng runs to the doorway, stops and searches the fields. Tall shadows stand motionless at the palisades – all along the palisades. The fields writhe in the rain and wind – the sea of weeds unfurls, but the shadows stand like mannequins.

Yíng watches them.

The door slams his face and knocks him down. A man grabs him, throws him out to the storm. The rain buries him and he sleeps.

Agents cut into the chapel and find Lumeina in the aisle. Her little body is balled up and her face is at her knees. Her ponytail slides down her side like a black boa.

"Girl! Stand up!" an agent says. He steps toward and casts a light on her.

Nothing moves.

The leaks cease, the wind stalls, the rain stills. The agent orders soldiers to take her. Two men proceed, surround the girl and lean down.

They stop.

The agent waits for them.

He waits – they remain stooped and solid as statues.

"Wey! What's the matter with you two? Pick her up!"

The agent nears, traces black bands with his flashlight – follows the bands from her scalp, up their bodies and strangling their throats. The thistle vines loosen and the men slump into kowtow.

His flashlight falls from his limp hand. He rushes in.

Backup follows close behind.

...

Outside, Yíng rises from a puddle and stumbles to his feet. He faces the palisade – sees jade blades slice soldiers into salad. The pineapple plants rush the underbrush, swift and silent – their faces masked and their heads in ornate helmets.

Yíng leaves the samurai to their art.

He turns around and sees the crippled doorway. He bursts into the chapel, peeks in from around the wall.

Sprawled in the aisle are two warm piles of men with crimped necks and flashlights. Their throats remind him of raw sausage links. He turns out and vomits sour tomato stew.

Yíng returns inside – avoids the ground meat, hurries through the chapel, hurries into the halls. He turns a corner and stops.

Far ahead, three men stand with their backs to him. The
agents look down the hallway and the hallway stares back at
them. The three scream at the spectre:

"Who are you!"

"Leave us!"

Yíng watches their flashlights probe the shadow and
disappear. Their lights only darken the darkness. He
remembers abyss.

"Aside! Or we open fire!"

"Aside!"

Their firearms rattle the hallway – ignite the house with
firecrackers. Fissures span the walls like a net. A blur of
centipedes sifts to the surface and swarms towards them.
Their bullets shoot into the shadow and bite nothing.

Abyss approaches – smears near like a black burn mark,
an absence in the present.

The scar consumes their lights. They fire on – emptying
their rounds into emptiness. Yíng hears thunder while the
men scream. They ditch their weapons and flee the shadow.
They race from the dark. They see Yíng and Yíng sees them
flee nowhere.

"Boy!"

"Help us! Help!"

Yíng watches their legs move – but they do not move.
The men throw themselves ahead – leaping and crawling –
but distance stretches from their reach. They run and the
expanse runs swifter. Distance deserts them. They run until
their blood runs from their legs.

"Don't leave us!"

"Boy! You must help!"

The absence absorbs them. They seep into the scar
screeching like swine in a tar pit.

But their screams and echoes persist, on and on like in
an empty cave.

The shade snuffs their cries and stops before Yíng. It
stares at him and sees everything. The centipedes weave into
the shadow – flailing like the tendrils of a Portuguese man-
of-war. Its cold barbs rake Yíng's body.

Yíng glares into its black – dares the perfect blindness: "Where is Fei-Lumeina?"

The shadow falls like a curtain of ash, and the ash pile dissolves into the floor.

Yíng is alone in the quiet hallway.

He hears a forest of books shedding its leaves.

ORIGAMI MOMMY

60 The library is a heap of amputated spines, pages and covers. Lumeina sits in the leaves, hunches over a paper head in her lap. Fresh paper-cuts glove her fingers like scarlet lacework. Red fingerprints mar the yellowed pages – psoriasis over jaundice.

"Fei?" Yíng digs for her. He finds her folding, snipping, weaving and curving a book into a ball. "What are you doing? We have to get away..." He offers his hand.

Luu lowers her face to the ball and pats its bald head. She reaches to her hair, stirs her fingers around the strands. Yíng hears bananas tear from their stems. Yíng sees her hair tearing from theirs.

"Fei!" he shouts and grabs her hand. She shakes him off and grafts the hair onto the yellow scalp. Her hands leak red glue. Yíng watches and sniffs away his sobs, "I know you miss her – I miss her too, but we have to run-loh... we have to..."

She does not touch him – does not look at him.

Yíng leaves the library, wanders to a window and peers outside. The samurai and palisades are mulch.

"Boy! Stay where you are!" Men rush down the hall. Yíng turns to them.

"You have to jàu-ah! All of you! Get away!" Yíng shouts – waves them off.

"You know where the girl is! Tell us where she is!"

"What do you want with her? You have to go!"

"We'll go when we have her. Be a good comrade and help the party."

"She won't go! You must go! Or you will die!"

The agent holds Yíng's shoulder, "Little boy – the girl is your friend? I promise she will be fine, and we will be fine too."

Yíng looks at the man's eyes. His goggles mirror the hallway behind Yíng: Fei and a woman turn the corner and walk down the hall, filling the reflection. Yíng watches the reflection on the lenses like a small television screen in monochrome.

The agent rises with his hand on his holster. The others do the same.

"Girls – stay where you are."

Fei and the woman approach.

"Stay where you are! We are armed!"

They do not stop.

The agent mutters to Yíng, "Do they not understand? Tell them to stop."

Yíng stares down the hallway and does not move. He backs away from them – from everyone.

The girl and the woman finally stop. The agents proceed. Yíng watches the men proceed slow, slow and slow until they meet the Chúng family.

"What the Hell!"

The men scream.

They howl.

The origami woman embraces the men with her folds. Her paper gown drapes them – smothers their eyes and mouths. She disrobes herself into a whirl of fans and confetti. She mummifies the men and they fall to their knees. Her skin bonds to theirs and hems them in like shrinking iron maidens.

They disappear inside her.

Lumeina passes over the agents. She moves through the hallway – she finds Yíng.

He stares past her and eyes the squirming cocoons. The men moan like cattle and writhe like maggots.

Lumeina reaches for Yíng.

He backs away.

THE DENUNCIATION

61 There is no color.
No white.
No reflection.
Her eyes are an absence.
Her fingertips brush Yíng as he backs away. They stare at each other as he moves further down the hall – faster than she follows, faster and faster until he drowns into the distance.

He sweats to get away.

The men succumb to their paper caskets. The house stills. Lumeina hears Yíng's breaths – short and swift like a drowning person. She watches his skinny silhouette shrink into the grey doorway. She listens to his breaths scurry outside and melt into some place far and farther off.

The door shuts.

Its clap slaps her to her knees. She lowers to her shins and sits with the dark.

...

The door breaks open. Cold grey day douses her.

Luu springs to her knees but the silhouettes are not his.

The men throw her down with chains and nets. They search her with their cold gloves and clubs. Soldiers fill the hallway and house – shout at her to rise, but she trembles on and on and her lips are too silent.

They rip her off the floor and out of her home. She brings her hands together over her heart – restrains it from boring through her chest. Her ribs rattle against her steel cicatrix. Outside, agents and soldiers stare at the barefoot girl with long hair in a burlap gown. They drag her to a truck.

The rain rinses black ink from her hair. It drips and stains like black ghost blood. It clings to the soil, to the soldiers, to their fishing gear. The ink grins and winks her way.

Behind the veil of weeds and palisades, Yíng watches the men bind her and carry her off. The house empties and brightens.

Flames raise the dark house to the clouds – and the flames smear the sky with streaks of sunset. The violet and blood-orange smoke burns day into night – burns through the night as Yíng weeps. His tears are thick and bitter.

EDEN'S ASHES

62 The ground has a heartbeat. It beckons him to wake. Yíng spreads his fingers open in the grass – spreads his body on the flowerbed. He opens his eyes, but dried paste crusts them shut. He picks the scurf off his eyelids – peels them from his lashes, digs his eyes up from night.

Tree limbs hang limp under the weight of fruit. Ripe tangerines smear the air with scent – they fall from their branches, bounce like tiny basketballs and vanish down the slope like setting suns. He smells blossoms in the garden. The fields bleed sweet blood. Breezes churn the leaves into avocado cream. Berries rain like hail.

A fruit falls to his palm. Its jade robe surrenders its blushing flesh. It beckons him to peck. Yíng tastes its gift and finds within a breath. He rises and the garden awaits – his every step sinks into velvet petals.

The house is now a black hill of flowers – its summit dressed with enough butterflies to fill a room. Yíng departs the lush palisades and wanders the field.

The mud paddies are azure fountains. The pavement is plush moss. The trees droop with ornaments. The ducks are cirrus stranded on land. The dust powdering his feet is gold.

He stops at the base of the hill – its black sand is warm under his soles. He scoops an orchid from the ashes and watches it stretch for sky – open its buds with a yawn. Its white petals unfold, its roots grope the open air, its leaves uncoil. He remembers newspaper wings doing the same. He rubs the flower's flesh – reads its veins.

Yíng tucks the plant back in its nest and moves up the hill. He wanders the patchwork of flowers – maps a long row of blue petals, squares of pink, halls of violet and rooms of yellow. The butterflies summon – open a pathway as he walks through the backdoor.

Some blue petals wither black. Yíng crouches to the dark flower patch and pats the black mound. A pair of goggles pricks his palm – its frame is wrung into wire and its lenses nowhere near. Yíng backs away from the mound – steps over into pinks, violets, then into yellow flowers. He knocks a boulder with his heel. It echoes at him.

Yíng digs for the boulder, finds a glass jar beneath the ash bed – a jar the size of a watermelon. He rests the glass melon between his legs and pops off the lid. Hot air peeps out and cool air peeps in. A bundle of cardboard sits inside like a roll-cake. Yíng lifts out the moist caramel layers and spreads them out under the sun. Charcoal ink wrinkles on the paper, mostly as handwriting* until he sees two feet standing side by side – one young, one old. He touches the footprints – the ridges of ink.

He counts the toes and the lines – the curves.

* See page 246 for the transcription of the discovered handwriting.
WARNING: TRANSCRIPTION CONTAINS MAJOR SPOILERS.

DREAM GIRL

63 They rest her feet against a cold mirror. A cold light stares and flashes at her feet. They repeat the scan with her hands, and then with the intricate cicatrix lassoing her body. Then they leave her on the cold table, leaving to stare at a sheet of her feet.

They count her toes and lines, *her* toes and lines – her curves and *her* curves. Four footprints stand on the lit photograph – a foot in each corner, like a mother teaching her toddler to walk. They spread one sheet of feet over another and seek.

They seek through her blood, sweat, urine and tears. They inspect hair, skin and nails. They map her eyes, chart her skeleton, navigate her flesh. They compare them.

They observe her through the electric two-way mirror. They watch their last mermaid.

They watch her from where she cannot watch them. They watch for many moments.

They touch one another with smiles and handshakes as they leave the aquarium.

One man lingers – hidden from her.

He touches the mirror where she lies on the other side of the pane: she fits in his fingertips.

He sighs and looks away. His breath fogs the window – the pulse in his hand nudges the glass. He turns, exits and leaves behind his handprint.

...

A seat waits for him in the meeting room. Others applaud as he makes his way around the wide table.

"Doctor Wòng! What an accomplishment – without you, she would have been lost years ago. She is a masterpiece."

"Except, she cannot speak."

"An improvement!" the men chuckle.

"How very wise it was to have them kept in their natural habitat for observation."

"Though it is a waste the original did not survive."

"But the two *are* identical. Her flesh is *her* flesh, her blood is *her* blood, bones are *her* bones–"

"Yet, she is her own..." Dr. Wòng mutters.

"What was that?" They lean in their ears.

"Never mind – nothing." He shakes off the thought.

"Good – the party has also willed to relocate the girl."

"To an off-shore facility."

"Secure from the restless mainland."

"Our work can continue there uninterrupted."

They watch Dr. Wòng. He holds his face in neutral.

"If that is best for the girl, very good." Wòng says.

"It is – best for the party."

"We will start relocation immediately."

"The party has decided on a secure area?" Dr. Wòng asks.

"Yes – the middle of nowhere."

...

Lumeina sniffs – a strange odor piques her, surrounds her, reminds her.

She stands on her toes and leans up, fits her hand in his handprint. She strokes the mirror – brushes the reflection of her long hair. She fingers the reflection.

Her actual hair parts around her fingers.

She rubs the mirror where the blue gown hangs from her body.

The gown moves too. She remembers the shade of blue.

Her hand sweats onto the glass and mists the mirror.

The mist spreads and cloaks all the walls.

...

The doctors return to the lab and gape at the whitewashed glass. Dr. Wòng sees where he had placed his hand – and sees hers. The others see only hers – a hand in white sand.

"Turn the glass off."

The current ceases, but the glass does not clear.

"Check the power."

"What is this?"

Dr. Wòng approaches her hand.

"The cameras are dark. We can't see."

"Open the vault."

A splinter sprouts off her thumb – shoots like a bolt of lightning. The fracture shimmers across the mirror. Dr. Wòng peers as more bolts span the glass wall – lacerate the clouds.

Thunder follows.

Then shards of hail.

The lab coats bleed. The shower of glass scourges the room. Sirens prolong the thunderclap. Nothing touches Dr. Wòng. The chaos stuns him still. She stands with her hand raised to his handprint – high-five.

"Lumeina!" Dr. Wòng hurries, clasps her hand and checks her. Her eyes close when he sees their absence.

She faints.

He catches her, peels back an eyelid and finds health.

Agents storm into the laboratory. They see the mutilation and they see Dr. Wòng holding the sleeping girl. They see his colleagues strewn like wads of stained and spent gauze.

THEY SAID THEY ARE GOD

64 The wide table hides under a mask of loose documents. Dr. Wòng slouches and stares at the teak surface peeking through. He folds his hands around a pen and just sits. He squints in the bright room.

A party cadre sits nearby with pen and open black book.

"Dr. Wòng – I've written what you report, but... understand it is not understandable." The cadre drops the book into Dr. Wòng's view. He does not look. "Perhaps the glass malfunctioned and a power surge caused the incident?"

The cadre waits for an answer.

"Please cooperate with us, Dr. Wòng. Your unbroken loyalty to the party has been proven time and again. The party respects you and honors you."

"You suspect I sabotaged..." Dr. Wòng says.

"Impossible. Do not disrespect the party by assuming such groundless conclusions."

"I mean the party no disrespect."

"Good – I will log that you merely misspoke out of... stress." The cadre makes a note and reaches for Dr. Wòng's hand. "Doctor, I will not log this: but you said the observation glass is bullet resistant. *That* I have logged. But how are our superiors to accept that bullet resistant glass shattered at the touch of a girl? The party does not find amusement in tales like this – especially after having to accept that a fanatic female and her spawn rigged enough booby traps to eliminate dozens of soldiers and agents..."

The cadre leans back, "Let's just log that the electric glass was improperly manufactured – in America. This will allow your work to proceed." He turns the logbook right-side up for Dr. Wòng – moves his hand over the blank paper, "Very simple – just copy mine in your own words."

The doctor starts reading and rewriting. He stops after a few strokes, "But this is not accurate... not true..."

"You claim it is a lie? You claim I fabricated?" The cadre leans in, "Doctor – how can what you say be true, when we say it is not?"

PALMISTRY MYSTERY

65 His fingertips read her toe prints. The charcoal crust sands his skin – keeps crumbs of him in its wrinkles. He washes their feet with his wet hands. He watches their feet dissolve in his sweat and stain his fingers.

Yíng whispers prayers to each toe, feels the face of each toe, wipes the face of each toe. He kneels in the flowerbed – ignores days and nights – and just whispers. He whispers with his lips, whispers with his sweat, with his fingers, with tears and hunger.

He writes on her charcoal sole.

...

Her toes wriggle and curl. Her body shivers – ripples like a body of water. The massage reaches out and wraps her, seeps through her skin, through her flesh and follows her blood to her heart. Her next heartbeat quivers. Her next breath is a sigh of tremors. She smiles and listens to him.

She pulsates with him – chants with him.

She feels his wet fingers rubbing her foot – tapping and stroking into her. With each stroke, she hears his pulse in his fingertips. She reaches to tap him back. She grasps for him with her toes. She touches her sole.

...

Yíng stops. He scratches the beetle off his foot, but it clings. He pulls his leg up, looks for the bug crawling from toe to heel.

There is no bug.

He watches a spectress finger his foot. He feels the warm touch reach into him – whispering his name.

He hears her.

Ying looks around him. He looks.

He looks on.

He looks back to his foot. He looks at nothing and asks, "Fei?"

The touch persists. The shape of her flesh, the firmness of her bone, the breath in her blood is hers. It is her and he is here and she is not. Ying kneads his sole with his palm, smacks his foot on the ground, gnaws it with his fingernails – but the single stroke becomes two, three, four and more until he hears his name again:

Ying – why did you scratch me? It hurt.

He freezes. Breezes bury him in petals and sun. Her strokes move from his sole to his palm. She tickles and spreads his sweat:

Why did you leave me? It hurt.

His open hand catches his tears. The droplets trace the lines of her words – bolding them.

SURPRISE REPLIES

66 Luu stares in the dark – stares at the silhouette of her open hand. She wiggles her fingers – sees the black octopus swim in the black sea. She pokes the creature's head and tattoos it with black stripes: *Ying...*

She adds more stripes: *Why are you ignoring me?*

The octopus droops its arms – floats like flotsam.

"I was afraid."

The octopus pops open like popcorn.

Of what?

"Of you..."

Afraid of me? Why?

"You hurt all those people... you were scary."

What did I do?

Silence.

Ying? What did I do?

Silence.

YING!

The room screams at her.

The explosion twists her ears and illumines the cell. Broken light bulbs smoke like ghosts hatching from eggshells. The bulbs crackle and burn orange like forest fire. Lumeina sees her hair – violet and violent in the firelight. The room is snared in its barbed wire web. Its tresses are rigid and clotted with red grease. She reaches for a tangle of vines and they retreat – some into jagged shadows and some into her headdress.

Lumeina sits up on the firm bed. Straps, buckles and straitjackets are splayed open and dangle off the side. The straps are snapped, the buckles are shrapnel, the jackets are shreds. She slides her feet to the floor and steps into puddles of glass. The shards tinkle like ice. She lifts a large piece to her face, inspects her hair:

Upon her head rests an ebony crown with obsidian gems, braids of black jade, tassels at the corners. She searches the diadem and cannot find where it ends – where her hair begins. She tugs a tassel and feels the tug on her scalp.

She drops the mirror and searches her blue gown – notices black strands wound around its fibers, constricting its weave.

The blue blackens.

The strangler fig crawls from her collar to her knees. It slithers against her, redresses her as an empress. It laces up her back. It leaves her hair draping her like a dress.

The room leans forward, then sways. It bellows, shudders, then hums and numbs her feet. Lumeina finds a steel door flapping like a lame eyelid. She leaves the room of smashed glass. The corridor is the same.

She braces along the wall and steps into the distant dark.

DECEPTRESS

67 The corridor smells like Mother. It hums like her, speaks like her. She smells Mother's breath mix with her words: *Remember – outside is dangerous... outside is not for you. Remember...*

Lumeina slows her steps. She releases the wall and trails a puff of sizzles. Her feet slap the floor like drops of rain. Her lips smack at the flavors of tangerine yolk, avocado cream, rice clouds, bubble beans and crispy cubes.

Her hair moistens under warm lips. Fingers slide beneath her headdress and cuddle her scalp. She follows the fingers into the kitchen, to the kitchen floor. Beakers – full, emptying and empty – clink against her steps. Lumeina's breath steams in the iced room. Her feet melt the floor and leave tracks of puddles.

She follows the fingers to her mother's arm, follows the arm to Mother. She touches her mother and waits. She waits and hears her stomach lose patience. It mumbles – ruffles like an empty bag. Her eyes adjust to the dark room and she sees a smile on Mother's white face.

She touches the smile – traces the purple lips. She dips her fingertips into the mouth and strokes dry teeth. She touches her mother's brow, her chest, then her shoulders. Lumeina rests her hands on her mother's breast and searches for her heart. She finds deep trenches between her ribs, cratered peaks and a vast caldera in dormant tundra. The calloused land crumbles under her palms. She draws in the sand: *Ah-Máh – where are you?*

She lowers her face to her mother's neck. Her lips move, her breath flows but her speech does not sound. She etches scars into the drought: *Why did you go?*

The flesh responds, rippling under her lips and hands. Her mother moves – her white skin opens for bulging black vessels. Lumeina lifts away – hears the caldera murmur. The parched plain cracks like terracotta. Shadows emerge from her navel like snakes from their den. They touch Lumeina – cling like hookworms. They murmur into her blood: *Outside is dangerous... outside is not for you – stay inside. Stay here with us. Stay forever.*

Black maggots pool and spill from her mother's mouth. They trickle out her ears and from under her eyelids. They flow like diarrhea. They stain her porcelain face. They murmur more and more.

Lumeina flings them off her body. They clutch her legs and become flesh slippers. They grope her hands and arms. They hide in her headdress. They nibble the scars crowning her breast.

WHAT ARE YOU!

The worms flail like tiger-leeches: *Your lovers we are!*

She flees the room – stomps the slippers into black ink. She rips handfuls of them off her body – flays them like patches of hair. Their teeth brand her flesh with fresh incisions. The bite wounds pucker their lips, laughing and moaning. They howl for her – screech like nails against chalkboards and cicadas in heat:

Stay with Ah-Máhhh!
Don't leave us!
Abandon you we will never!

TRADING FEET FOR FINS

68 The corridor ends with an ascending stairwell. Her feet feel for each step. She races up the throat. Wind rushes up past and down around her – tossing her dress and tassels. She climbs – passes all doors and new smells: strange waxes, strange fires, strange soups and strange smoke, but she stops for nothing.

Dank breath fills her lungs. She casts open armored doors and the sky flogs her with ocean wind. The sky screams and the sea writhes like sheets upon the bed of lovers. Lumeina falls to her side and watches the deck lurch. She lurches with it.

The ocean stones her with cold water. The rocks crumble into slivers of ice. The needles stick her and suck her warmth. Water slicks the floor, sweeps it smooth. The sea beads on her imperial attire and rolls off like caviar.

She catches a rail and stands with it – gasping with the panting Pacific. She looks into the ocean, into the typhoon, the tsunamis. She looks through the storm and sees a woman on the water – her feet dipping the ocean like ballet in the rain. The waves and wind buckle around the silent woman.

Lumeina fills her eyes with the woman: a veil thinner than moonlight rests on her head and a robe lusher than rainforest cradles her body. Her black hair *glows* black – a bright black that burns the dark. Her complexion is dawn after a storm. Her smile rivals beauty.

Lumeina reaches out for her with arms and tears.

She leans over the rail and leaps into the sea. She runs to the woman – her steps toss waves and foam. The ocean rolls under her stride – stretches the distance between her and the woman in moon-blush. She throws her arms ahead, flails her legs, but the water clasps her toes. The headdress splits into a

medusa of wires and the black dress shrinks into a corset.
Both embalm Lumeina into a solid silhouette.

Lumeina falls to the waves, seeps into the black water –
buried alive.

The woman leans into the sea and swims with Lumeina.

The ocean above lulls as Lumeina's breath lulls – stills
as she stills, wanes as she wanes.

REPLY DEPRIVED

69 Yíng slumps into the flowerbed – holds his left hand in his right. He stares as the veins turn cold – bluer than horseshoe-crab blood. His palm is wet and glares in the sun.

He strikes her name on his palm again – fast and firm enough to light matchsticks. He listens for her and feels for her – for anything but her silence.

Yíng tries again and again.

菲?

Again and again.

菲...

He smothers his cold hand with his face. Seawater puddles in his palm – he mumbles into numbness, "Ah-Fei – you're scaring me again... mõh-lah..."

All he feels is cold.

...

Moments pass...
months pass...
years...

...

"AND SHE INCREASED
IN WISDOM AND IN STATURE..."

INSPIRED BY: LUKE 2:52

LITTLE MISS MERMAID

70 She sleeps in black – black as blindness. Legions huddle around and whisper into the dark. They dangle small lamps and juggle small flames. They float and grasp and they all whisper about her. They first whispered when she arrived, and they whispered as they watched her mature, and they whisper now to a young woman.

They sleep with her – on her body and under her. They hide in her hair and in her dress. They whisper with her breaths. She keeps them warm and they keep her close.

Lumeina sleeps in the dark – on and under their nightlight bodies. She rests with her cheek and belly on the bed – with her back under the care of tender masseurs and masseuses. She sleeps until she sees carnelian.

The black corrodes. A light douses her in its glimpse. It sees all but her. The masseurs scatter from the spotlight and the masseuses duck from view. They flee as the orbs drift by.

She lifts her eyelids and lifts her arms. She stumbles out of bed, notices stars hovering and touching her. Spiral galaxies lock arms with her. Constellations morph into new faces. The night sky smiles, frowns, blinks and winks like ornate lion-dance heads. She scratches her eyes and follows the shining orbs drifting further away. They drift in a circle.

...

The grey sand is a graffiti field. Worm and eel tracks, shrimp and crab tracks blemish the bed. Ship and whale skeletons atrophy from mountains to mounds to mud. The seafloor is a world awake with sleepwalkers.

Footprints catch their eyes. They peer out the dome window. They inspect the video monitor. The human prints are clear and remind them of strolls on the beach.

They measure the prints, capture the prints, share the prints and track the prints.

They find a princess.

They turn and see her standing alone in their searchlight. They gaze and she gazes back.

They watch her dress sway. Her hair glints at its tips – lit like live fiber-optic strands. She steps to them and they watch her walk the seabed. She nears the dome and wrinkles her nose against it. She notices – recognizes the stars on the hull – the yellow on the red. She claws the decal, drags her fingernail across its face:

斃

Her tousled hair leans back and assembles into a headdress. Her face brightens white but her eyes dilate into black holes. Her lips sometimes touch and sometimes not, and her body is unmoving. She is still for many moments.

Moments pass as worms slather the searchlights with their bodies. The divers watch the dark sea consume them, shell and all. The glow of squid, jellies, fish and eels flicker into a lightning storm.

She spreads her hands on the dome, watches the divers disappear behind the glass. She feels them tremble within, their skulls resonate their screams, their whimpers seep from the hull and mumble into the depths. The sea sneaks in to meet them. Strands of her hair bare their leech-fangs and slice through.

The strands slip in and leave bite marks. The hairs gather over the divers and drown them in black. The sleepwalkers gut the tortoise. The sleepwalkers make them sleep. Outside, she watches the empty steel shell rise into darkness.

TEMPTRESS

71 A black finger takes her hand – twines itself around her fist. It lifts her arm and kisses her wrist. It beckons and she follows. It escorts her through the dense dark air. Lumeina watches fireflies and purple clouds waft by. She watches them waft while she stops at the edge of abyss.

The chasm swallows the horizon. She steps back from the mouth's blistered lips. She turns but her escort grips her. It reaches up her arm, binds her neck and murmurs into her ear. Its wide grin glows papaya-pink against her cheek. Its toothless jaw nibbles her ear. Its nibbles echo into her stomach. Her stomach nibbles her from the inside.

She stoops to a stone and scoops it off the seafloor. The rock melts in her palm – turns brown and sweet. The pelican eel licks the honeyed mud off her knuckles. It guides her hand to her tongue.

A song pauses her heart. A hum longs for her from deep in the dark. She listens for it but her stomach snarls – snuffing the song. The black eel murmurs more. It dips its tail into the mud and touches it to her lips. Lumeina tastes cocoa.

But the pink grin takes the cocoa. Lumeina searches for it but finds nothing around her. She stands on a sliver of land crumbling into morsels – stands on the tip of a forked tongue stranded in gaping jaws. The eel slinks to her legs and walks her to the edge. It soothes her with strokes and purrs – promises that her steps will land. She smells the mud in the distance – across the bottomless moat.

Lumeina's feet reach into emptiness. She sinks into the dark and strikes a black bubble. The bubble shivers under her weight – flickers like a cloud of lightning. She hops off the jelly and steps to another. It wakes under her toes, flails its tentacles to balance. Lumeina dances over abyss. She leaves behind islands of thunderheads, sprites and halos.

Spectre steps raise Lumeina to a peak. From the height, the eel lies with her headdress while she gazes out over the wilderness below. Glowing squid ink and arms, twinkling scales and fins, neon fangs and suckers illustrate the world's flavors, wealth and wonders.

She stands in the center. Creation peers up and adores. The summit sprouts a throne of corals, and the eel is her crown. It spawns tassels. She touches the sea anemones and they clasp her fingertips and toes. They call her their queen and goddess. The nightlights lift her to the throne and rest her upon cathedra. They sing for her and she listens.

She lets herself and she lets them.

DRAGON'S TRIANGLE

72 The crane dangles the dive pod like a yo-yo from a finger. The ship's crew weighs the vessel, scans the hull, inspects the door and counts the incisions in the glass. They read the message carved on the party flag. They review the divers' recordings.

A party cadre removes his glove and touches the blade marks on the dome. The strikes resemble leech bites. He reads their lips – traces the three incisions. He knocks on the dome and peers into the vacant cockpit. He grasps the hatch and others assist him. The bolts withdraw.

They search the cockpit, find nothing but three long strands of black hair – a strand coiled on each seat. The cadre snatches a strand, but it slips through his grip. It slips through his fingers and his fingers slip from him.

His fingers sit idle on the cushion.

His hand flails – sprits blood like a syringe. He stumbles out the hatch and screams – waves his hand and everyone backs away. He runs rings on the deck and stains the floor with red shoeprints. His eyes dim – his head bobbles until he scurries past open gates. His shoes smear a trail into the sea. Everyone watches the spume smother him.

They slam the hatch.

They raise the crane and hoist the submersible. They dangle the pod over the water. They drop the yo-yo and sink it into the sea.

They spray away his shoeprints. They jettison all records.

ORIGAMI ORACLE

73 Butterflies in a bag, in a row, in a huddle and in his hands – he sits in a hive. The paper is like python hide. He presses the leather between thumb and finger – creases it and it greases him with ink. He tears the movie poster, folds the celebrity faces, bends them into a body, coaxes open wings. Its span hides his face from the city.

Coins tap his bare toes.

"Wai! Sèí Dài-Loòk-Jèí! Make trash somewhere else!"

The coins are bottle caps. A man sweeps dust onto Yíng. The origami scats like tumbleweeds.

Yíng gathers his bag – stuffs it with his paperwork. He hops into his sandals and slaps off down the street. Pedestrians make way for the leper.

Yíng turns into an alley. He checks his pockets for bulges and bundles. He leans up and sighs at the skyscrapers. Violet clouds flowing over the towers blush blood-orange. He slumps against a wall – watches the chameleon sky. The buildings lean with the bay breezes. He remembers watching trees sway the same – less rigid but just as lit. He watches them appear in his sleep.

...

The trees drool sizzling sap. Bark blackens, crinkles, curls off the trees like phantom fingers peeling rancid bananas. Flames grind the fields, the palisades, the garden into black pepper. The fire broils the house into brittle crusts. The butterflies burn into incense, rise up as a swarm of ash.

One escapes and flops through the smoke – its charred wings tipped with embers. It crop-dusts hot cinders before incinerating in Yíng's palm. Its cremains stain his skin with a shadow. The dark strokes settle into him:

菲

New flames rise behind Yíng – from far off, from down the dirt road. The fire smothers the night with light – smothers the cries, the screams, the village.

None escape.

...

Yíng wakes. He rises to his feet. His palm is clean but warm with the strokes. He traces the touch – writes her name.

BURIAL AT SEA

74 She holds his hand – his warmth in her palm, his voice within reach.

AH-YÍNG!

Black swells the anemone seat – the glowing throne becomes shadow. The aurora holds its breath and the night sky hides its luminous eyes. Blindness drowns Lumeina. Absence gags her. She grips for Yíng – keeps him close.

Shadows grip her instead – seek to enter. Trespassers mine into her. Serpent-stars bind her from face to foot. Osedax-worms penetrate, take root. Vampire-squids bag her, haul her off the summit.

They sink her into the throat of the trench.

Hagfish rush into the horde. They seal her within them, suspend her in their cesspool. Their sputum coagulates into a tomb.

Lumeina tears away and they pursue. She spits and they lick. She kicks and they kiss. She slaps and they sap her. Her hair strips her and rips the cicatrix from her flesh. The serpent-stars pluck at the embedded beads, the zombie-worms pierce and burrow, the hagfish suckle.

But her steel scar persists. Her moles repel the molesters, refuse her immolation, resist extraction. The assault merely shines, buffs and chromes the beads. They are warm with her, shine with her.

They are scalding to the dark.

The molesters fan out from her – exploding like a depth charge, lingering like a smoke bomb. They avoid her, but stalk her as she descends through the trench. Lampreys circle her and murmur, sleeper-sharks watch for sleep, and the eel puckers its papaya lips at her. They all watch from arm's length.

They all wait.

Her feet meet bottom.

She breaks from the dark slime. She peels herself free and her pearls cast the seabed in moon-glow. Bony trees with fanged leaves and barbed vines, fountains of sulfur and wells of tar, and paths of spider crabs greet her at the garden gates.

Lumeina's eyes wander the site of the feeding and their feed. Everything is gnawing and clawing in the graveyard. Everything lolls in the shadows of skeletons.

Everything stops and stares at her. Flesh without eyes spawn eyes to see, bodies without arms spawn arms to grasp. They surround her – immure her within a great wall of hunger.

SEA OF THRENODY

75 Song floods the dark. Chant ripples through the absence. The hum of hundreds routs the thousands. The song washes the water, the weeping overwhelms bulwarks and weeds graves. Their echoes dust off the expanse – beating it like a rug.

The shadows forsake Lumeina.

They burrow into the sea mire – dive into the quicksand. They poke holes into the mud – pock it like denuded and chilled chicken skin.

Lumeina's cicatrix brightens in the deserted depths – the moon is uncloaked. The choir hovers overhead like continents of cumulus. Lumeina listens to the raining serenade.

They squeak for her, squeal for her, click, clap and tap for her. They have bass solos and the ocean is their cathedral. Lumeina resonates with them – sings with them. She flips her feet and ascends to them.

Moonrise.

The clouds warm into shades of indigo and cerulean. Their tails pat the sky with sleepy strokes, their breasts drip with their lullaby, their warmth nurses the cold. Lumeina joins the traveling family and they welcome her into their troupe.

A brow leans up and gives her rest. She sits on the swimming island – watches the seascape undress its veiled body of hills, veins, wounds and plains. Hot breath sighs to the surface and chapped flesh bleeds into the wilderness – clotting into land. Snow hovers everywhere like falling flakes of bread. Crumbs cling to Lumeina and coat her with confetti. On her lips, she tastes all sweetness.

And she sees all sweetness.

She sees him against a sky of twinkling starfish. Lumeina leaps from the troupe and sinks to the sky below, sinks to Yíng's arms – open and wide. She shuts her eyes and gasps. He holds her – secures her in his silhouette. His body consumes the moon.

The whales circle from far atop. They whimper for her, but their echoes do not pass Yíng's many arms.

The tips of his limbs scribble on her. Suckers pluck along her flesh. The couple drifts high above the stars – her corona like a pearl clutched within dragon talons. She spreads her fingers along his shifting muscles. Eight voices murmur to her skin: *Fei, Fei, Fei, Fei, Fei, Fei, Fei, Fei...*

She absorbs every word.

They descend.

Yíng – I'm sorry I was scary. I don't know why I did that... I will never do it again.

Yíng brings her closer. His pulse is swift against her. His suckers cup her ears: *But you must do it again. I was a coward – but now I see it was your only way. You must avenge your mother – must seek out the agents and destroy Mr. Wòng.*

The voices reverberate in her skull – she hears them in her thoughts.

Mr. Wong? But he is not –

The murmurs interrupt: *He is nothing but evil. Do not be deceived like your mother – she trusted and see where she is now! She trusted and forgave – and see it has led to her murder! Betrayal...*

Lumeina opens her eyes.

They press a strawberry to her mouth. They brush her eyelids down.

Fei – let me show you what I know... let me show you your mother's secret.

THE GIRL WITHOUT HER NAME

76 Yíng brings Lumeina's feet to deck. She spreads her toes on the strong surface. He clings to her – dangles weightless around her – he leads her across deck with two arms guiding, four arms clinging, and two sweeping the path before her.

They come to a door. He retracts his arms into his head and places her hand on the latch. She opens and they enter.

Serpent-stars scatter from sight. Under shadow cover, the stars mold their limbs into men's legs, arms and heads. File-clams embed themselves as mouths – their beards weave into surgical masks. Moon-jellies cloak the men in white lab coats.

The doctors wait for her.

Yíng lifts Lumeina's eyelids. The clean and gleaming hallway squeaks under her feet. She stops dripping seawater and starts dripping sweat. Yíng pats her dry and walks her down the hall. The chilled air tightens her skin and the electric lights whiten her. They follow the doctors into a room with women asleep on tables. Agents watch from behind glass walls. She hears them breathe, speak and think.

A doctor rubs her mother's flat belly. Lumeina leaps to her, but Yíng keeps her. A needle breaks into her mother's garden and seeks the tree of life. They pluck unripe fruit. The doctors seed the fruit with familiar seed found in her mother's blood.

The needle returns to the garden and seeks the fountain. They sow the fruit and watch her grow. They sow all the women's gardens – each woman's fruit seeded with her own blood.

"Dr. Wòng – if your procedure succeeds, you will be greatly honored as the genius you are." The agents speak into a microphone. Lumeina stands motionless at the sound of Mr. Wòng's name.

"It *will* succeed. The procedure has been perfected. Within a generation, new brides will be ready for our sons."

"Beware of boasting, Wòng. The party keeps its promises and expects you to keep yours."

"It is not a boast – it is the truth. Not a promise but a guarantee. Forced conception is as sound as forced abortion. With enough support – even refined and perfected brides can be made from these simple, flawed, religious fanatic mermaids... refined, perfected into my masterpieces."

Dr. Wòng turns to Lumeina.

They all turn to her.

The surgical masks flare their whiskers. The moon-jellies pale into clear mantles. The serpent-stars reach out from their cloaks – they embrace Lumeina with their striped arms.

Ours you are... our masterpiece.

Their tattered lips moan like toothless jaws – their tongues swim like flatworms. Lumeina grasps for Yíng but he is gone from her side – caught in a net of tentacles.

"Fei! You must avenge your mother! Avenge me! Avenge us! He does not love you, He is the traitor! Betrayer! Avenge yourself!" he screams at the faceless bodies as they smother him.

Her eyes become abyss and her hair sears the water into steam. She torches the lab's façade and it bares its dereliction. The ship rusts into mulch. She cries silent screams – her gaping mouth breaks her face half open. Creatures fall on her from all directions. Her hair lashes, beheads and quarters them. She climbs from the ghost ship and stumbles into the middle of nowhere.

Vast void surrounds Lumeina. She finds nothing but balls of fangs hemming her in. The barren is a field of urchins crawling to a dish. She stands on the shrinking clearing – it closes in on her like a contracting pupil. A durian springs to her leg. She dodges – escapes with a grazed knee.

Her hair braids into chains and scourges the urchins.

All pop off the floor and shoot for her. Her hair lengthens, swings, hammers and demolishes the ocean bed. The water warps, the land splits – raw magma burns the urchins into meteors.

Lumeina gathers handfuls of molten mud and flings away. Her hair catches fire and throws light across the ocean floor. The strands scorch the seascape. She lifts her arms and the illumined sea rises from its bed. It levitates and hesitates before her. The muck shrivels into desert, the creatures wrinkle into raisins, the burnt urchins spice the lava. Lumeina forces the sea higher into its attic and inundates the seafloor with daylight. She walks its sands, traverses its ravines – tracks the tick of propellers.

The tick slows into stillness. She glares up at it – stares through miles of sea. She waits and it remains.

She leaps, cuts into the ceiling of sea.

The ocean drops and stomps the seafloor.

Lumeina rushes up through the water like a giant squid – her hair trails her head and lashes her ankles. At the edge of the deep, her silhouette attracts ambush. Leviathan launches at her, widens its jaws and closes on her. Lumeina is trapped between a throat and a boulder.

Teeth crack along the whale's gums. Lumeina curls against the rock. The sperm whale bites again.

The boulder opens its fins and keeps Lumeina close to its belly-armor. It slaps the water and shields her against incisors. The sea turtle jets from the whale's mouth like a spat seed.

Lumeina jets from the turtle – full speed to the surface. Black gives way to grey gives way to blue gives way to white. The ship's white hull is within strike.

The sea turtle eclipses the hull.

Lumeina splatters onto its shell. Her hair flattens against it like squashed spider legs. She sprawls on its back, falls unconscious and dozes through the rest of the ride.

GUARDIAN

77 Fish parade by in full costume and array. Some wear fur and others don manes. Some sashay and others flow like a marquee of balloons.

The turtle basks on the promenade. Its veins swell under its heated shell. Its heartbeat knocks like a shy guest. Lumeina sleeps on the turtle's back – draped in a blanket of fine kelp and coral jewels. Her hair is shortened to her shoulders and piled around her head like a silk pillow. Her skin fills with sun and her stomach fills with tremors. She rubs her cheek on the shell. The scales against her face wrinkle their lines into familiar words: *Hungry-mah?*

Lumeina tilts her head, nudges the scales with her nose. She pushes herself up and sits on the turtle-bed. Her palms read the animal's writing: *You are safe here. I am your guardian.*

She opens her eyes – reads the jade tiles. The shell's pigments and ridges adjust. She presses the shell, finds scars and sutures on the sugar-apple rind. She responds with her fingertips: *What happened?*

The turtle leans its head back and looks at Lumeina. Its eye is a monk fruit, its beak is curved into a smile at the corners. Lumeina touches its nose with her hands. It blows bubbles onto her fingers: *You were being scary again.*

Lumeina traces the smile: *You stopped me...*

The turtle bobs its head.

Thank you for doing that – where am I?

You are in the desert.

It's a very wet desert... Lumeina squints her eyes: *You look very old... how old are you-geh?*

I am very old. We are the same age.

Lumeina squints her eyes even more: *Well, old turtle – do you have a name-mah?*

I am your guardian. I am yours to name.

Lumeina sits back. She crouches low to its shell, strokes a story onto it: *My mother once told me about a mighty guardian with a mighty shield like yours – very old too – but there's a big problem...*

The scales shift: *What is it?*

It's a boy name... are you a boy?

The turtle grins. Lumeina scoots to his head, traces three characters down his brow:

彌
額
爾

Her strokes settle into the bald head. The marks stain his brow with an orange tint. He wears his name like a bandana.

SANCTUM

78 The turtle rises off the sand and floats Lumeina to a
kelp forest. He glides through the blue like a flying
carpet. She gazes at the oasis around her: bands of pygmy
seahorses, pods of dolphins, shoals of color, beds of wild
coral, fish dancing with flowers, and palaces fashioned with
animate bricks. The castles grow and surprise their guests
with new towers, rooms and walls.

The kelp forest is spirals of luscious noodles wallowing
in warm soup. Fresh vegetables and seafood hide in its
braids. Wonton dumplings idle and recline in too rich a sauce
to swim. Lumeina slides off the turtle's shell. She reaches
back and asks: *Mey-Keo... what is this place?*

Braille peaks up like welts on his shell: *This is your place.
You will meet them here.*

Meet who?

Your victims.

Scars hewn deep in his shield grate her touch. Mey-
Keo's flesh is soft in the armor's gashes. Lumeina gazes at the
aged battle scars – navigates the jagged grooves with her
fingertips: *Who did this to you-gah?*

Mey-Keo looks Lumeina in the eye. She sees no one in
its copper gloss but her. The turtle blinks and nudges her
with his nose – shoos her into the grove. She turns back only
to see him glide into the sky.

Bubbles spring from the seabed around her feet. The
tapioca pearls lift, whirl and wrap Lumeina in a chrysalis.
The drops of air cling to her – pop against her like
whispering lips: *Forgiven – forgiven – forgiven...*

She glances to her feet. Lobsters and crabs blushing
brighter than hot cinders, they approach in silent procession.

Lumeina crouches to them. Their scalded skeletons hiss. She
reaches for their burnt bodies, sits with them as they gather.
Fish with missing fins and tails – they float overhead
like maimed clouds in sunset. Others stagger with kebab
sticks impaled through their flesh. Some swim while their
scales and skin dissolve into the sea. Jellies shed their arms
from their heads and their heads from their arms. Brittle-
stars hold their limbs in rigid cruciform – the forest floor is
crowded with Calvaries. Whales – their hides calloused and
blistered – hum litanies from their loft high in the canopy:

KÝRIE, ELÉISON... KÝRIE, ELÉISON.
CHRISTE, ELÉISON... CHRISTE, ELÉISON.
KÝRIE, ELÉISON... KÝRIE, ELÉISON.

CHRISTE, AUDI NOS... CHRISTE, AUDI NOS.
CHRISTE, EXÁUDI NOS... CHRISTE, EXÁUDI NOS.

PATER DE CÆLIS, DEUS... MISERÉRE EA.
FILI, REDÉMPTOR MUNDI, DEUS... MISERÉRE EA.
SPIRÍTUS SANCTE, DEUS... MISERÉRE EA.
SANCTA TRINÍTAS, UNUS DEUS... MISERÉRE EA.

SANCTA MARÍA... ORA PRO EA.
SANCTA DEI GÉNETRIX... ORA PRO EA.
SANCTA VIRGO VÍRGINUM... ORA PRO EA.

SANCTE MÍCHAËL... ORA PRO EA.
SANCTE GÁBRIËL... ORA PRO EA.
SANCTE RÁPHAËL... ORA PRO EA.
OMNES SANCTI ANGELI ET ARCHÁNGELI... ORÁTE PRO EA.
OMNES SANCTI BEATÓRUM SPIRITUUM ÓRDINES...
ORÁTE PRO EA.

SANCTE IOÁNNES BAPTÍSTA... ORA PRO EA.
SANCTE IOSEPH... ORA PRO EA.
OMNES SANCTI PATRIÁRCHÆ ET PROPHÉTÆ... ORÁTE PRO EA.

SANCTE PETRE... ORA PRO EA.
SANCTE PAULE... ORA PRO EA.
SANCTE ANDRÉA... ORA PRO EA.
SANCTE IACÓBE... ORA PRO EA.
SANCTE IOÁNNES... ORA PRO EA.
SANCTE THOMA... ORA PRO EA.

Sancte Iacóbe... ora pro ea.
Sancte Philíppe... ora pro ea.
Sancte Bartolomǽe... ora pro ea.
Sancte Matthǽe... ora pro ea.
Sancte Simon... ora pro ea.
Sancte Thaddǽe... ora pro ea.
Sancte Matthía... ora pro ea.
Sancte Bárnaba... ora pro ea.
Sancte Luca... ora pro ea.
Sancte Marce... ora pro ea.
Omnes sancti Apóstoli et Evangelístæ... oráte pro ea.
Omnes sancti Discípuli Dómini... oráte pro ea.

Omnes sancti Innocéntes... oráte pro ea.
Sancte Stéphane... ora pro ea.
Sancte Laurénti... ora pro ea.
Sancte Vincénti... ora pro ea.
Sancti Fabiáne et Sebastiáne... oráte pro ea.
Sancti Iohánnes et Paule... oráte pro ea.
Sancti Cosma et Damiáne... oráte pro ea.
Sancti Gervási et Protási... oráte pro ea.
Omnes sancti Mártyres... oráte pro ea.

Sancte Sylvéster... ora pro ea.
Sancte Gregóri... ora pro ea.
Sancte Ambrósi... ora pro ea.
Sancte Augustíne... ora pro ea.
Sancte Hierónyme... ora pro ea.
Sancte Martíne... ora pro ea.
Sancte Nicoláë... ora pro ea.
Omnes sancti Pontífices et Confessóres... oráte pro ea.
Omnes sancti Doctóres... oráte pro ea.

Sancte Antóni... ora pro ea.
Sancte Benedícte... ora pro ea.
Sancte Bernárde... ora pro ea.
Sancte Domínice... ora pro ea.
Sancte Francísce... ora pro ea.
Omnes sancti Sacerdótes et Levítæ... oráte pro ea.
Omnes sancti Mónachi et Eremítæ... oráte pro ea.

Sancta Anna... ora pro ea.
Sancta Filoména... ora pro ea.

SANCTA TERESIA... ORA PRO EA.
SANCTA ROSA... ORA PRO EA.
SANCTA MONICA... ORA PRO EA.
SANCTA ELISABETH... ORA PRO EA.
SANCTA MARÍA MAGDALÉNA... ORA PRO EA.
SANCTA AGATHA... ORA PRO EA.
SANCTA LÚCIA... ORA PRO EA.
SANCTA AGNES... ORA PRO EA.
SANCTA CÆCÍLIA... ORA PRO EA.
SANCTA CATHARÍNA... ORA PRO EA.
SANCTA BÁRBARA... ORA PRO EA.
SANCTA ANASTÁSIA... ORA PRO EA.
OMNES SANCTAE VÍRGINES ET VÍDUÆ... ORÁTE PRO EA.

OMNES SANCTI ET SANCTÆ DEI... ORÁTE PRO EA...

Lumeina watches the persecuted procession. They do not take their eyes off her. She reads the crystal balls – watches how they died.

Forgiven – forgiven... they all breathe out to her – sending up undersea incense. They robe her in a gown of bubbles and song:

RORÁTE CÆLI DÉSUPER –
ET NUBES PLUANT JUSTUM...

* See page 255 for the translated text of the Litany of the Saints.

THE WHITE ROOM

79 Snow, then lava.
He blinks again.

Snow, then lava. He grips the padded frame of his white bed – his knuckles rattle under the stress. His body quivers like legs plucked fresh off an albino tarantula.

His white clothes, the white lights, the white floor, walls and ceiling, the white camera watching over him – he drowns in the white. His breath is quick – little nips of air. His eyes scour the white – flashes from side to side, corner to corner, white to white.

The lights go dark.

The room shudders with howling. His lungs bleat like haunted bagpipes. Chimpanzee, crow and walrus spew from his gut into the dark.

The lights return.

The howling calms to panting. The white blurs his eyes but he blinks not. They observe him from surveillance and they blink not.

"What has happened?" an agent says.

"He has gone mad."

"I can see that, but how?"

"Well, it's definitely not simply nyctophobia. He has been behaving this way since he was found. He will not tell what happened, or what he experiences – nothing. All he does is scream at darkness or at black objects. He does not respond to anything but the absence of light. Darkness frightens him into madness – the room must be lit enough so he can blink without seeing black. He does not sleep."

"How was he found?"

"The coastguards who located his research vessel – they reported hearing his shrieks from their ship. When they

searched the vessel, they found him hysterical in the
laboratory – screaming in the dark, screaming himself in and
out of consciousness. Mold had covered the room and began
festering on his clothes. They said he had been trying to set
himself on fire. He was the only survivor."

"Why is he bald?"

"His black hair terrorizes him – we clean shave him
regularly."

"Why not just bleach the hair?"

"We tried – it would not bleach."

The agent's eyes widen. "I will speak with him."

The doctors help the agent into a suit room. White
garments hang from the wall like rows of ghosts. The agent
waves off the garments.

"Sir, you must be in white, through and through. He
will not tolerate even the pupils in your eyes. He would tear
them out if he could." The doctors direct him to the suits.

"Alone – I will speak with him alone." The agent dons a
white lab suit and mask, then steps into the white room. The
light is intense and fills the cell with glare. The agent
approaches the bed, watches the man's sweat soak the sheets,
corrode the buckles, erode the bed.

"Dr. Wòng – do you remember me? We last met seven
years ago." the agent says. Wòng's face is blank. "I am Agent
Lau. I am aware of the mission you headed. The party has
sent me to recover you and help salvage your successes."

Wòng stares up at Agent Lau. He looks through him.

"Dr. Wòng, please. You know what happened. Tell me
what happened – what happened to the girl? Where is she
now?"

Wòng just pants and sweats. The agent tries again but
there is no response. "Dr. Wòng! Can you hear me? Do you
understand what I'm saying?"

Wòng stares – his eyes snap into all directions. The
agent lifts his hand and pulls it over Dr. Wòng's face –
casting a subtle shadow. Wòng freezes in the shade.

Lau clamps his hand over the doctor's eyes.

The doctor thrashes against bed and belts. He beats the room with ruckus – wrestles and twists like a crocodile. The agent presses harder until banshees jam needles into his ears.

He removes his hand from the hot kettle.

CITY LIFE

80 Ying lifts a pot off the fire. He balances the bruised tin handles with charred chopsticks, fills wrinkled foam bowls with steam. Everyone sits and watches their supper bathe. The noodles grow supple in the spa and the soup grows fragrant.

"I haven't had one of these in decades-loh..." a man says, then sighs.

"I love these – thank you, Ah-Ying..."

"I hate these! Full of *mei-jing* and salt – but thank you. Definitely better than dumpster diving."

"You get by alright selling those paper puppets."

Ying bows his head. He serves the noodles.

"It's a shame you're stuck here with us... you should escape. Leave the city."

"Leave the country! You still have your youth – you can make it."

"You still have your feet!" The man pats his stumpy ankles. Everyone chuckles.

"*And* your hair!" An old woman slaps the man's head, "Old Man Tong's shiny gong would give away his position any day!"

"Old Lady Soh forgets that I'm her faithful husband of thirty years."

"I don't forget anything – I know I can say anything *because* you're faithful!" She leans against her husband and smiles.

"Ah-Ying, please don't spend on us like this anymore. Save up and get out."

"You've been here too long-lah."

"Yes, get out while you can."

"I can't..."

"You told us you came into the city to find someone. What if she's not here anymore? Maybe she has gone on... think about it-lah."

"Hong Kong is not what it used to be – not free anymore, not even free to use Cantonese without party permission." Old Soh shakes her head.

"You never told us much about her. Don't mean to be nosy – but we can help you... we want to help. What is she like? Who is she?"

Yíng stares into the steam. The moisture condenses on his eyes. He finishes his noodles and etches on the foam bowl. The chopstick squeaks as he engraves. Chatter stops.

They search his chicken scratch:

她是個秘密

"Ah-Yíng... but it's no secret that whoever she is – she would want you to escape too."

Yíng sits up in the circle of squatters. He shows them his palms, "I felt her today. I haven't felt her in seven years, but I did today. She feels the same..."

They search his hands like palm readers.

"Look... you know we're all open to miracles. Nothing is impossible for God... but we still don't understand–"

"I don't understand either. I've never understood why I can't let her go – why I won't. All I know is that when I wrote her name on my palm – she held my hand. She was... reaching for me."

They search his face like lip readers.

"I know how she feels, I know her touch... I know but it's difficult to explain."

"Then what happened?"

Yíng pauses.

"Black... then I felt darkness – everything went blind. My touch, hearing, smell... all went black, like I was drowning in cold. I could taste it."

They all stare at Yíng. They cross themselves – their hands swift like martial artists ✛, their whispers softer than litter rustling down streets.

LEFTOVERS

81 "Psst! Wey... Ah-Yíng!"
Yíng gathers the empty foam bowls. He hands them off, then follows Old Tong to the side. The two huddle in a corner. Hidden from others, Tong pries apart a seam in his jacket, feels for the joey in the kangaroo pouch.

"You're not the only one with secret powers... I want to give this to you." Tong draws a mashed packet from the jacket's flesh. White sand flows in the plastic pack.

"No – Ah-Bok... I can't take this – I don't use it."

"Shh! It's not cocaine – it's better than that." Tong shoves the pouch into Yíng's hand, "It's the last thing I have from a priest long dead... you've probably never even seen a priest before, right-mah?"

Yíng shakes his head, peers into the powder. It twinkles like diamonds in the low light.

"It's exorcized salt... and the priest was no ordinary priest – he was a pope. When he visited the mainland decades ago, the party ambushed him with its thugs. That was the end of the peace – the Easter Massacre – that was all before your time..."

Old Tong takes Yíng's hands. Yíng follows teardrops to the old man's eyes.

"It happened right here – Hong Kong... on the last day of his visit, and at the last place in China anyone would've thought it could happen. I was in the cathedral on that day – now they've turned it into an orgy cesspool."

The man's tears disappear. He closes Yíng's hands around the packet.

"Please – take it. I've had enough salt from the noodles anyway."

Yíng chuckles – stops himself.

"It's okay, I like being a comedian." Tong pats the young man's shoulder, "I have another joke – but you have to know some English. Do you?"

"Someone once taught me a little..."

"Okay – what does the party call the Holy See?"

Yíng shrugs.

"The Holy Sèé! Get it? Sèé? *Shit?* The Holy shit?" The old man shivers with laughter.

The young man does not.

"Ai-yah... I'll be damned to Hell for that blasphemy..." Tong sighs.

Yíng laughs.

PASSOVER

82 The air is dank with breathing and sweating. The concrete floor is damp and garbage fires fill the space with black and orange. The abandoned factory rusts, crusts and creaks.

Bundled magazines pillow Yíng's head. He sleeps in the middle of a field of tired people. The warehouse floor lifts and falls – lifts and falls through the night to the song of snores and sighs.

A plastic bag ruffles beside Yíng. Papers in the bag shift as an origami wing machetes its way out. The butterfly flits into the air, stays low and hovers to Yíng's nose. Its fashion-magazine complexion fades into starlit midnight.

The butterfly flicks and itches Yíng's nose. Yíng twitches, scratches and sniffs. He turns to his side and slumbers on. The wings crawl to his cheek and stand firm. It brushes his face but he sleeps through it. The butterfly braces, aims its rear at Yíng's nostrils, and then croaks. Its paper body buzzes from the release.

Yíng opens his eyes. The butterfly launches and he sits up. The firelight catches its black wings. Yíng rises – watches the creature beckon. It does not wait and folds into the darkness.

Yíng hops across scrap piles and leaps over sleeping people. His quick footwork echoes in the warehouse. The echoes fade as he chases the wings into a stairwell, up to the roof.

The butterfly waits on a ledge overlooking the factory courtyard. Yíng nears its night-sky body. It darkens its complexion until it disappears into the shadows. Yíng darkens with it – his rags and flesh surrender to the night.

Flares set the warehouse windows ablaze. Broken glass channels the flashes into shards of lightning. Agents and soldiers storm the open doors and silence the snores. They drag people from their tatters and line the yard with men, then women, then children.

They take the women and girls.

They control the population of men and boys.

Trucks fill with bodies and the night is quiet.

Yíng spots the bronze gong.

"Ah-Bok!" Yíng cries – silences.

The old man glances up and smiles. He traces a cross in the air with his head – a nod and a turn ✚. A fist crumples the gong. Old Tong slumps from the herd.

The stairwell rumbles with boots. The factory's warped skeleton whines. Soldiers fill each floor, fill each truck with more and more. Yíng feels the stampede near the roof. He tucks against the ledge, finds nowhere to leap and watches the stairway vomit agents. They swarm the open space, march along the ledges and bleach the roof with searchlights.

They search. They scour.

They pass Yíng by. They see through and step through him. Their cameras find no heat and their hounds smell no man. They leave the roof and leave the factory emptied.

Yíng sits against the ledge. Day breaks against his back and fills the courtyard with dawn. Rags droop in the morning wind – limp, lurching, searching for their missing bodies.

DOLORÓSA

83 Drops of summer rain trickle from above. Tears cascade and burst with weeping and humming. The droplets bathe Lumeina in warmth warmer than her own breaths. The tears sweeten the sea. The chantress steeps the ocean into tea.

The blue whale rests high above the canopy – higher than the others. She sleeps in the heavens – swims in a sea of her own tears and milk. Her sheets are the waves and her bed is the deep. The other whales sway aside and honor her. They shush and silence in her presence.

Her heart pours its song into the waters. Everywhere, her pulse resounds and resides – swaddling everyone and clasping every heart. Lumeina's body trembles: her bones tingle like tuning forks and her marrow echoes like flutes. Her hair tinkles like strings under a bow and her blood undulates like water in water drums. The song massages her throat and coaxes her lungs:

> stabat mater dolorósa.
> juxta crucem lacrymósa.
> dum pendébat fílius.
>
> cujus ánimam geméntem
> contristátem et doléntem.
> pertransívit gládius.
>
> o quam tristis et áfflícta.
> fuit illa benedícta.
> mater unigéniti...

The bubble-gown lifts Lumeina off the seafloor and to the whale. Seven spears, each longer than Lumeina, protrude from the whale's breast and jolt with each heartbeat. Lumeina nears a harpoon – the whale's pulse throbs through the wound. She swims close to the whale and touches the source of sorrow: *Why do you weep? Who did this to you?*

The whale yelps. Blood drips down the spears and fades into milk.

Lumeina floats from the spires and finds the whale's face. She looks into her eye – gazes until the woman's eyes gaze in return. She holds Lumeina and bathes her with her bright black hair. The spears are seven gold swords – warm and gleaming. Lumeina leans her face against her – listens to her heart behind its veil of flesh. Her fingertips whisper to her heart: *Why did you leave me? Why did you leave us?*

It was not I who left – but you who left me...

Lumeina turns up to the woman's face – crowned with the sun and blushed with the moon.

My child... I weep for you... we all weep for you. The sea is our tears and the sky is our sighs.

Lumeina touches the woman's lips: *I don't understand...*

The woman brushes Lumeina's hair, kisses her brow: *My little one... my little light... when it is your hour, all will be made known to you. The truth will cause you sorrow, but know that you are always with me, and all that is mine is yours. I am yours. And when your hour ends – please come home... please choose home.*

The kiss blinds Lumeina. She sees sun and moon meet, feels ecstasy and peace embrace, and nothing but beauty. She hears music and silence sing, tastes all sweetness and breathes nothing but beauty. Lumeina touches her own brow and traces the lips. The remnants of the kiss warm her hand.

She traces the kiss as she sinks to the sea forest – tracing and tasting the entire time.

DUC IN ALTUM

84 Her feet land on Mey-Keo's shell. She rests on his back – entranced and still. The turtle descends through the blue as she reclines. He sets her gently on the sea-forest floor in the midst of the other creatures. They begin to depart.

Lumeina rubs her cheek against Mey-Keo's shield. His heart is strong and slow. She scratches his armor: *Do you know her?*

Yes – she is our Queen.

She is beautiful... I want to be like her...

Mey-Keo leans his head back with a grin.

Mey-Keo... where is everyone going?

He shakes his head. The scales on his face fill with tattoos: *Lumeina – your time left with us is short. Soon you must be put out into the deep. Remember us when you are in the desert... remember us when your hour comes. We have never forgotten you – He has never forsaken you.*

Lumeina breathes. Her breath sears her nose and chest. Seawater seals her throat and floods her blood. She flails from Mey-Keo's shell, shivers and slumps. Her panic and pain stings him through his armor.

His grin becomes stern. The turtle flips her like stir-fry in a wok. She dangles in the sea, her hair hovers like hijiki. He fetches her locks in his beak, tucks her between his fin and belly-shell, keeps her close to his heart. He jets off the ocean floor – cuts through water, shoots to shallow and strikes for surface.

A writhing array of nails hurls towards the pair. The bear trap targets Lumeina. It draws its fangs and bites on.

Mey-Keo's shield blunts its spikes. The crown-of-thorns starfish anchors onto the turtle. It regurgitates its gut over

Mey-Keo, eager to slather the girl into its sack. The turtle spins – spins until the bur ball falls away. Mey-Keo torpedoes ahead.

A barrier of barbs coats the surface. Jellies and Portuguese men-of-war smear the sea like oil spill. Stingrays, sea kraits and blue-ring octopi patrol the border. Mey-Keo eyes the horde and plows into them shield first. Fangs, stingers and needles hit the shell and ricochet.

The pair breaks surface. They go airborne.

Lumeina rests pressed to Mey-Keo's breastplate. He coasts the air, soars, then smacks water and surfs the sea's face. Sunrise ignites the waterway before them – a rip current of golden mercury leads to shore.

The turtle backstrokes beside the riptide – pummeling attackers into the torrent. He twists his neck to see ahead. His fins slice and dice the legions into bait. Their red, blue, clear blood flavors the savory sea.

Hammerheads and great whites sweep into the plague. Their jaws rake the waters and clear the way for Mey-Keo.

He crashes to shore, throws sand into the dawn. It falls like snowballs and snowflakes. He rolls Lumeina onto the beach. The sand is plush like flour and warm like baked bread.

...

Lumeina wakes. Sour water drizzles from her lips. She coughs, pushes herself off the powder and it billows up under her breath. She sits and the dust settles. Her hair is dry – it drapes from her nape around her body like a gown. She wanders the beach – alone and surrounded by day. She finds a mound, stumbles to Mey-Keo's side.

Teardrops course from his eyes. She catches them in her palms – fills her hands and they leak down her arms and spill upon her lap. The turtle lies on his back – his head in shreds and his shell in shards. Lumeina adds her own to her handful of turtle tears.

The blend stains her fingernails with black strokes. It puddles at her feet and smears her toenails. She reads the stains: *Fei-Lumeina – do not weep for me. We will meet again. Go seek the truth. Seek him who seeks you.*

Her guardian's words are warm and fluid under her nails. She keeps them close to her gaze as they fade.

She turns from her hands and the turtle is gone from shore. Mey-Keo's subtle blue shadow sloughs apart in the surf.

Lumeina thrashes into the waves, chases the silhouette and stands in its warm waters. She stands there – watches the sea try to splash the sky and the sky try to dry the sea.

WEEPING WOOD

85 The butterfly takes space again. Its wings block sun and its body blocks view. Yíng sees his hands and body emerge from hiding. His shadow is where it should be – and it is his. The butterfly dashes into the air, makes for the stairs. Yíng follows.

He follows the wings down the steps, through the corridors and across the warehouse. The factory is cold and the autumn day is weak. Yíng finds only sheets with moth nips, only stains where his friends had slept. Smoothed concrete marks where feet once walked – day in and year out.

The butterfly does not wait. It leaves Yíng – leaves the courtyard and leaves the site. Yíng catches up to it. He strolls with the wings – they shade his head from the sun. The squatter camp is a ghost village. Tents, boxes and mouse holes stare off with blank eyes and gaping mouths. Crickets, flies, mosquitoes and frogs roam the neighborhoods. Yíng passes through.

He stops.

Footsteps continue. He listens to the quick footwork – the feet scurry past factory doors and down long halls. Yíng watches the butterfly sift into the dusty factory. He turns to the door and peers down the corridor. The butterfly is gone. The dust on the floor is blemished with a trail.

"Wey! Who's there?" he calls out and listens to silence. He traces the steps with his own – paces with the short stride. The little toes and little feet lead him to a descending stairwell. He calls down the well and hears his echo fill the chamber. Yíng turns away, then turns back when he hears a boy.

"Who's there? Where are you?" Yíng says.

"Down here... help me."

Yíng descends the stairwell. His eyes adjust to the shadows. He grips the handrail until it ends – until it leaves him wandering a moonless night. "Where are you?" Yíng calls, "are you hurt?"

"I can't find my mom and dad..." the boy whimpers. Droplets ripple puddles. Feet scrape rough cement.

"Let me help." Yíng tracks the boy's voice. It echoes.

The echoes swell and surge – stranding Yíng on an isle of noise. A pandemonium of sniffles, ripples and shuffling feet boxes Yíng's ears. He listens for the boy but hears everything else.

Yíng catches a night-crawler under his foot. The leathery body squirms and salivates. Hundreds of feet smack the floor – hundreds squeal and sprawl off. Yíng freezes as the frenzy leaves him in solitude.

"Where are my mom and dad? Why did they leave me here?"

Yíng listens. His eyes adjust again. Silhouettes appear – a man and a woman. They hurry through the dark – the man holds a baby boy close and grips the woman's hand. She bundles the baby in old clothes, pins his name to the bundle and tucks him into a basket. She kisses her child's feet and rocks him to sleep.

The man digs into the ground with a shovel. He breaks the dirt – guts it like a watermelon. He packs the hole's walls, lines the nest with sheets. They lower their son into the burrow. They lay logs across the opening, piling logs atop and around. They leave him and wait for night to pass.

The man helps his wife upstairs. She rubs her rounded womb and weeps.

Men emerge from the night and douse the house in searchlights. They separate the man from the woman – the woman from the illegal child. They thrash through the home – find nothing of value. They nail all its doors and windows – they seal the casket.

They sell the house and the village to others.

Others break open the sealed doors and windows. Another man and another woman bring another boy into the house. They hear the logs cry for the forest.

TURTLE TOUR

86 Pebbles bump Lumeina from behind. They float like little soy-sauce dishes paddling through the surf. A trail of baby sea turtles streams from the beach – queues into the water. Lumeina wades past them – careful and gentle as they flit by.

She tracks the turtles to their nest. They emerge from the sand one at a time – crawling from their crater without a peep. They pay no attention to her, nor to her shadow or feet. Their young flippers tickle her toes and leave wrinkles on the shore. Hundreds of them struggle in their nest below – sifting the sand under her soles. She follows them with her eyes, ears and touch. She sits and counts and cheers them on.

...

A final newborn finds its way to the surface. Its body is half that of its siblings. Lumeina waits for the little rock – watches for it in its womb of sand. The hatchling wrestles up the valley and rests at her foot. Its pipsqueak heart taps Lumeina's baby toe. She raises the turtle and carries it to the waves. The water laps it up, but its flippers cling to her.

She holds it in her palm – strokes its head.

Lumeina turns and the turtle turns. She steps this way and it scoots along. Whichever way she moves, the turtle adjusts to face inland – its head raised and nose pointing to the city. Lumeina follows the compass – holds it level in her hands.

DISTURBING THE PEACE

87 The turtle leads Lumeina from the sea to the land. It guides her through the parklands, boardwalks, bridges and gardens. People watch the strange girl in a strange dress strolling barefoot with a turtle turning in her palms.

Traffic and highways and bridges and skyscrapers – none of the sights, sounds and stares stop her. She walks through and past the city's richest streets, sleekest buildings, slickest automobiles and fashions. Nothing snatches her from her guide. Yellow brick roads, towers of Babel, limousines and palanquins with riders in suits and gowns of silk – nothing halts her. She strolls along in her spider-silk dress and nothing catches her eye.

Nothing – until the murmurs surround her.

Lumeina looks to her belly. It trembles under her glance, but it is not alone. She turns to others who tremble – the dozens of men who lay in the alley, clutching their guts to keep them from crawling off. Their stomachs croak like a bog of frogs.

She sets down the turtle. It waits for her. She approaches the nearest man – his eyes wide and his mouth speechless. They all watch her touch him.

His hollow gut moans – his body rings empty beneath the rags. Lumeina lifts the man's arm – his blood is slow and his sweat is fetid.

He does not move. She looks into his eyes and sees he cannot.

"They don't feed him. He can't fight so they don't let him eat."

Lumeina turns to the man who spoke.

"You're not from around here, are you? You should leave here – it's not safe for you. They will take you... they've taken all our daughters." The man nears, "And they make our sons fight each other for stolen brides."

Lumeina reaches for his hand. He does not offer it – he backs away from her grasp. He shoos her, "Please, before you are found here – you must go."

"Hurry!" they whisper. "Leave the city!"

"And don't come back!"

Lumeina stoops to scoop the turtle but cannot find it. The men fall quiet and slump into their corners. They watch well-fed and well-dressed men surround her.

"Little chick looking for her pet?" a man asks. Lumeina sees him from the corner of her eye – dangling the shell by its leg. He shakes the pendulum at her. She does not turn to him. "What are you doing here? Walking your turtle?" He tosses up the hatchling, catches it and crushes it like an egg in his fist. He peels off his glove and flings it to her feet. Shards of shell and twigs of bone cling to the empty hand. The man raises his arm, twirls his fingers and turns away.

The other men close in on Lumeina. They grab her. She elbows a man – sinks her elbow into his chest and strikes his heart. Its blood smothers his lungs. He sags from the others.

They jump her. She twirls, tosses her hair. Strands fan and burst into a blur. Fresh sliced faces and bodies fall to her feet. She stomps out the vortex. The blades re-sheathe, the whirlwind reweaves into her dress.

The man with one glove turns back. The girl stands over the well-dead men. He draws his firearm, "Sèí-Géi! You messed with the wrong triad!"

The hungry men watch his bullet shatter before her – it bursts into embers. They watch the girl stand her ground. They see other bullets disintegrate into cinders. Molten flakes powder her with glowing snow.

The clip clicks empty.

Lumeina peels the bloody glove off the ground. She finds its owner while he reloads and jitters. She looks into him. He sees the absence in her eyes – black as blindness.

His peace leaves him.

His sight leaves him. He flees in circles and flaps his wings. He howls and his howls fill the alley. His shrieks send everyone running – including the cripple. His lips gape and keep gaping.

Lumeina thrusts his glove into his torn mouth.

He goes mute.

VIGILANTESS

88

Applause.

Color returns to her eyes. She finds the clapper leaning against a telephone pole. He smiles and comes forward. His dark glasses hide his eyes.

"Amazing – I've never seen anyone like you. Those thugs finally got what they deserve."

She straightens up. He offers his hand with a grin, "My name is Hòu Jí-Min – and you are someone who can help, if you–"

Her stomach interrupts him.

"Let's talk over lunch." Jí-Min takes her hand and they leave the alley together.

...

Dishes await her on her left and dishes wait to be cleared on her right. Jí-Min just watches her appetite – the way her lips part and moisten, the way her tongue lathers, the way her cheeks stretch and rest, they way her neck pulses with every swallow. He outlines her hair, traces her flesh under the dress – it glistens like rain in the night.

He does not touch any part of the meal: clouds stuffed with pink shrimp, crisped turnip cakes, golden taro nests, plush rice rolls in sweet soy, glazed phoenix feet, blossom dumplings with orange pollen, chicken hidden in leaves, fluffed tofu pillows, brittle noodle bundles, spiced calamari, egg custard pies and silken pudding.

He pours her another cup of chrysanthemum tea. The server replaces the pot with another. She finishes off the last bamboo steamers.

"So you haven't told me your name yet..." Jí-Min says. He waves off the servers. They seal the door behind them.

She rests her chopsticks and leans towards Jí-Min, removes his sunglasses and places her hand on his face. He does not move. He closes his eyes. When he opens them – he feels her looking deep into him.

Too deep.

He blinks away – shakes his head, "So you can't speak?"

She takes up the chopsticks again – they clink in her fingers.

He nods, "You can't speak..." he takes out a pen and paper, "can you read and write-mah?"

She empties her teacup. He waits. She makes him wait for nothing.

"Well, none of that is really important anyway. What's important is that you can help protect this city from other thugs. Hong Kong is rotting – but with your help it can all be better. The police here are corrupt as the criminals, maybe more."

Jí-Min plucks the sticks from her fingers, puts her hands in his. She stares at their hands. "Please Miss... those poor hungry men you saw earlier – they need you. They've been forced to be gladiators – fighting for their clothes, their food, and then... for their sisters, daughters, or brides."

She stares on.

"Will you help?"

No answer.

He returns the chopsticks to her.

A Different Dress

89 Lumeina stares out the vehicle windows, pokes the air conditioner vents, wriggles in the leather seat and nudges the speaker with her toes. She parses the vibrations, reads the grain and hears the animal, feels her flesh cool – then regain warmth, and watches the skyline pass by.

Jí-Min drops a photograph on Lumeina's lap. The man on the paper stares back – his face is a freckle-mask.

"*That* is the worst man in Hong Kong. We're visiting him first. His name is Teng Sèú-Pìng. He controls more..." Lumeina hears Jí-Min, then hears him fade off. She wanders with the stereo, spies with the song as it choreographs the cityscape. She sways in her seat until Jí-Min plucks the stereo button.

"Did you hear what I just said? Teng is a very dangerous man."

Lumeina gazes out the window. The vehicle is stranded in traffic and the view is perfect. She watches a black dress hang in a storefront – alone and longing for a body. She grips the door handle and swings it aside. She leaps from her seat, hurries across the street, slips between bumpers and hops the curb. She does not hear the screams shouting after her.

The tall window pane looms over her. She steps toward the showcase of gowns and dresses – she presses her hand to the glass. The crystal is thick. She slides her hands to the black dress. She traces its silhouette and closes her fingers around it. The hem flutters.

Jí-Min darts through traffic – glancing and running. He glances at Lumeina, then at the street, then back to Lumeina, then at the dress – then at the dress on her body. It hangs no longer in the storefront, but dangles from her shoulders, hugs her figure, brushes her knees.

He slows to a stop. He watches from the street.

Horns squeal.

He wakes from the daze and scurries off the road. His steps to Lumeina are slow.

She watches her reflection in the clean glass – her handprints the only blemishes on the pane. She fixes the dress, her hair fixes itself – the strands loop and curl and shorten.

Jí-Min stands and sweats in place. His shirt darkens a shade.

Moments pass.

She plays with the small pocket behind her, sewn close to her waist.

He clears his throat and stutters, "Ready?"

Lumeina watches him in the reflection. She nods.

CASUAL CASUALTIES

90 Agent Lau inspects the men's faces – shred into
pleats. He flips their flesh like the pages of a book.
The cuts are sharp and straight and all the same. He looks at
the slivered beets wallowing in their broth. Crumbs of
contact lenses, glasses and teeth glint in the puddles. Lau
turns to several bound squatters.

"Someone tell me everything."

The men do not lift their heads.

"Hear me? Who did this? What did she look like?"

The men glance up.

"That's right – I know it was a girl. She belongs to the
party – and if we don't find her, everyone will have faces like
these!" Lau lifts a triad head into view and shakes it. The face
flaps like gills, slaps like wet rags.

A call comes in for Lau.

He stands fast.

He grows rigid, presses the earpiece deeper.

...

They lift her hands from the glass. The film peels back
and holds her fingerprints in place. Agent Lau counts them.
He meets the shopkeeper inside the store.

"Has anyone else seen the surveillance record?"

"None."

"Good."

They enter the store office and eye the monitors. Lau
waits for Lumeina to make her appearance.

"Here's when she first comes into view. At first I
thought she was like any other window-shopper, but then I

noticed she was only a commoner. Watch closely as she strokes the glass..."

Lau watches.

Lau sees.

The dress follows her fingertips – dances in sync.

"It's not the air conditioner – we don't have vents near the windows."

The dress pops off its mannequin and pops onto the girl. Lau nears the monitor. The shopkeeper rewinds the video.

"The camera doesn't catch what happened here. One second the dress is there – the next, it's on her body. I couldn't believe it myself. The video doesn't skip – it just... doesn't catch what happened-jeh."

Lau controls the replay himself – rewinds and rewinds again. He backs from the screen and zooms in. He slows it down and speeds it up. Every adjustment yields the same result.

"When I finally ran out to look – she was gone."

Lau sees Jí-Min creep on screen. He clenches the monitor until the display ripples.

Another call comes in for Lau. The display bruises and oozes in his grip.

DERANGED MARRIAGE

91 The double-doors open to the suite. Lumeina follows Jí-Min into the chilled room. The thick carpet embraces her feet with each step. She remembers wandering the garden.

Flowers line the windowsills. Fruit baskets line the countertops. Drapes line the view. Lumeina smells the flowerbeds and ripe groves. She touches the horizon.

Jí-Min spreads apart the wide windowpanes. The sky rushes in. The sea gushes below. Lumeina inhales clouds and sun. She takes in the afternoon.

The panorama snaps shut.

"Enough-lah – don't want to waste all the air conditioning."

Lumeina looks at Jí-Min as he walks away. He moves several bags stacked at the doors. He sets them at a couch and peeks into each with a grin. He cradles and coddles them like bundled babies. She approaches.

"Well done! All this will finally be put to good use-lah." Jí-Min keeps his eyes on the bags. He flips through pages of color – pocketing books of purple, red, brown and yellow. He notices Lumeina standing idle.

"We'll go shopping! I'll teach you how to use this." Jí-Min slaps a bill on her hip. The rigid banknote crackles like rice-paper. She lifts the slip to her face and follows the gold papier-mâché. She plucks the designs with her fingertips – probes the note's body. The paper is strong, firm, crisp. She smiles.

He snatches the bill from her.

"What are you doing? You'll rip it!" He pockets the yellow. "Lèi – you'll want to wash up now. You smell like men." He leads her to the teak bathroom, starts the bath and

gathers towels for her. "You know how to use these, right?
Toilet, faucet, lights, fan, hair dryer, shower, tub, bathrobes?"
He points to everything and she just looks along.

He pats the hooks by the door, "Just hang your dress
here. I'll get it washed for you." He leaves and closes the
door. He shakes his head, waits on the other side.

The door bumps into his back. Lumeina's arm pokes
from the door crack – handing him her dress.

BLEEDING BEAUTY

92 The water dissolves the salt off her skin. Her hair fills the pool with kelp. She lies in the bath – flavors it. Her fingers wrinkle like tealeaves and her pulse taps the water. She listens – her ears just under waterline.

Falling droplets ring out. Her breaths are clear and alone. Her knees, breasts and belly rise like shy isles. The still water laps along the tub's edges. The sounds sing her to sleep. She dozes off, slips into the bath.

"There's nothing in there-gah!" The water blackens into absence. Abyss opens around her. Up is down, then left, then right is up before becoming down. She falls through the dark – grasps with her hands and toes but nothing clasps back. Abyss swallows her.

She falls through clouds of rose tea. Her hair whips like flags in a typhoon. She bursts into night sky – her legs kick past the moon and her arms sweep a third of the stars into her hair. The ocean below folds itself – furrows its face at her.

The sky peals into daybreak. The black burns blue and the blue burns black. She scorches winds into cinder and clouds into ash. Rain sizzles down the sky's breath. She sears a path through the sky's body. It screams after her – its heart moans.

She strikes sea.

Tides spill out, up and over. The ocean splits, lifts and retreats. It rains in reverse. The sea sweats into the sky. She sees unseen land. The earth unveils its womb, its strong muscles, its veins and arteries, its hot blood.

She falls into a barren valley. The cliffs crumble as she enters. The mountains tear open with vines, forest, flora and fruit – all peeling apart to embrace her. The dark depth of the valley takes her in – breaks her fall, cradles her in a warm pool of marrow.

A body bathes with her in the fountain – an empty flesh, an absent person. The body is an anomaly – not seeded in the sincere, dignified way, not knit in the intimate way. It is born of blood, of the will of the flesh, of the will of man. Its lustful scent lures her like flies enticed by carrion. She embraces the young feminine flesh and the flesh embraces her. The two meld like wine in water.

The wine whitens her mind.

But the fountain trembles and collapses. The grotto constricts and the night sky shrinks. She presses back against the falling sky – touches the constellations, strokes the stars from dot to dot.

And the fountain sighs deeply and sings to her:

SALVE REGINA...

MATER MISERI... CÓRDIÆ...

She rests again in the intimate waters – sleeping, dancing, dreaming in the dark.

And when the song ends – the waters abandon her. The fountain ruptures and waterfalls pour from the valley, out the valley. The current takes her to meet Mother.

Lumeina rouses.

Bathwater drips from the ceiling and huddles in puddles on the teak tile. Her every breath is quick and heavy with humidity. Droplets trickle down the walls, down the curtains, down her body. The wide tub is empty of water. Warm grenadine slicks the porcelain and pinks her complexion.

There is beauty in the blood.

ACUPUNCTURED

93 Pinholes freckle the faces and bodies. The holes are pierced clean through clothes, skin, muscle, nails and bone. Agent Lau inspects a handgun with his flashlight – the light fills the hundreds of dots bored through the steel. Other agents flood the space with construction lamps.

The bunker is dusted with broken bulbs, punctured furniture, punctured floor, ceiling and walls – and bullets poked into crumbs. Lau picks a stray bullet off the floor, rolls it between his fingers. It flakes into sawdust.

The agents search the room. Their shadows follow along – hovering overhead, against the walls and underfoot. They sweep the area with photographs. Camera flashes bleach and fill the room with an indoor lightning storm. Agent Lau watches the shadows mimic their masters. They mime perfectly.

But they do not disappear under the camera flashes.

Lau turns a lamp to the photographers. They shield their eyes. Behind them are their shadows – arms down and heads up. The men move out of the way.

Their silhouettes do not.

The men watch the stains blacken under the lights. They stare at the blots – approach with their lamps and search the dark. No one speaks. They say nothing about the still silhouettes, nothing of their bodies casting no shadows, nothing of seeing nothing but absence.

An agent drops his camera. He panics.

He snatches his eyes – picks off his eyelids, pinches holes into the thin flesh, "I can't see!"

Lau watches the men around him – their eyes wide open and shrieking. They pry their eyes out to see. They stumble and grope with eyeballs clear as peeled lychees. They draw their firearms and empty rounds into the walls.

Lau stares at blind men shooting blind. He watches the live-action cartoon spectacular. Men rush into the walls like spooked swine into the sea. They implode into the brickwork – their bodies like statues of black ash, their only remnants like shadows burnt into masonry.

Lau watches everyone disappear – one by one across the room. The men's cries echo incessant from the stained stones. The walls weep.

Lau nears a screaming stain. He touches the perfect shadow, but brick touches back. He listens to the cries – so present, so alive. He backs away, plugs his ears.

He hammers the blacked bricks, but the cries continue. Then bullets gnaw the walls, gnaw until Lau's clip empties, but the howls persist. The howls follow Lau into the room opposite the wall. He throws open the door.

Quiet.

The shadows move without their masters. They shift like black sand on a white beach – they creep like ink bleeding through paper. They meet Lau with grins, then with faces, then bodied.

Lau slaps the light switch but the stains remain. They fill the bright walls. The shades consume and spawn. They seal the door and blackout ceiling and floor.

"What are you..." Lau says.

Thousands of little leech lips pucker from the bruised bricks. The stains speak together: "Many we are... very many."

They smile at Lau.

"What do you want?"

They wait for him to bow.

SHOPPING SPREE

94 Jí-Min waits at the counter in the ladies' department. The black dress is tucked under his arm. A young woman turns the corner, swings into her post.

"Yes?" she asks.

"I need clothes that fit the girl who wears this..." he lays the dress onto the counter, unfolds and spreads it slowly. The sales assistant smiles. She lifts the dress into her arms. Patches of the dress are warm to the touch.

"It's a beautiful dress... what colors does your girlfriend like?" She holds it by its straps. "Does she want more dresses? skirts? tops? jeans?"

Jí-Min squints and smiles, "Just casual clothes – boys' clothes actually."

"Boys' clothes? You two are planning something *special* for Moon Festival tonight?" she smirks.

"Keep this between you and me?" he says, "I know it sounds strange, but can you help?"

She smiles, "For a big-time triad thug like you? Absolutely."

"Great. So – I need some hooded sweaters, baggy pants, T-shirts... maybe some underwear."

"Panties? or..."

Jí-Min smiles, "I'm kidding you-jeh."

"Funny..." She rests the dress over herself – models with it clinging to her chest, "Oh! It has a pocket-méh? Very unusual for a dress like this..." She slips her fingers into the fold.

"It fits you," he says, follows the black curve along her body. She smiles and presses the dress close. She motions him to follow.

"How much do you plan to spend?"

Jí-Min watches her lead the way, "Enough."

"What about this-neh?" she asks, lifts a white hooded sweater into view. "It's my favorite – if I was a boy, I would wear this. The orange seams and zippers are cute." She toys with the pockets and laces.

Jí-Min watches her toy – watches the black dress slip down her body. "Hmm... seems to be just her size. Why don't you try it on for me? Help me decide..."

"Are you kidding again?" she laughs – hides her blush behind the hood.

"Please...?" He waits.

"My name is Wenna."

He smiles, "Please? Wenna?"

She rolls her eyes and sways to a stand of jeans, makes her way to the fitting rooms – picks more clothes along the way. He follows her with his eyes.

He follows her to the rooms.

LITTLE MISS ZOO MASTER

95 Lumeina steps from the bathroom. Her robe trails along like a wedding gown train. Her small body floats in its sleeves and skirt. Her wet legs and feet leave prints on the carpet. The prints fade as she wanders to a grey window mounted on the wall. She peers into the graphite sheen. She strokes the sides.

The window perks, shivers and blinks at her. Colors fill the gloss: forests appear, birdsong peeps from the frame. Lumeina gazes at the view. She dips her hands out the window, but it denies her.

The view switches. The Amazon disappears. A man talks and talks. She does not follow. Stories come and pass. She nudges the frame and the man disappears. A girl takes his place – stands alone in spotlight. Numbers border her body. The numbers increase.

Lumeina watches. The girl rotates on a pedestal. Her young face is tired and her eyes are down. She wears less and less as a man describes her more and more. They describe every part of her except her. Lumeina reaches to touch the tear on the girl's cheek. It glistens, dries in the spotlight.

Lumeina nears the couches, nears the bags – her gown fills and billows. The sheets of sunset beckon her to sit with them, beg her to give them bodies.

She kneels and sits on her shins. She throws her hair back, rolls her sleeves up, plucks a brick of yellow notes from the sack. The bills fall from the binding and pile on her lap. She sorts through the banknotes and counts up to the price of the girl. She keeps an eye on her rising value.

Lumeina grips a slip and refashions it. Her fingers are nimble, her folds are tight, measures are even. Her sweat seeps into the fibers. Her breath warms the paper. She presses the note into a butterfly. She blows it off her palm and watches it flutter free. She folds another.

And another.

More.

Soon, an origami cloud collects and huddles around her like a coral reef. Butterflies pop from Lumeina's lap like popcorn from a campfire. After she creases her final creature, she hurries to the windows and slides the panes apart. She sweeps out the suite and her origami tsunami gushes free like a waterfall. The purple, red, brown and yellow wings fill the sky like a wildfire.

Lumeina returns to the television with more cash in her lap. She keeps her hands busy while she watches and waits... waits... waits until the tsunami breaks into the broadcast. The man stops describing the girl and starts screaming. The butterfly bills fill the auction site and kill the live feed.

Lumeina smiles and turns off the static.

...

The suite floor soon crowds with creation again. She gives form to creatures with shields on their backs, with necks to hold their heads high, with enough arms to arm-wrestle eight men, with noses like hoses, with backs vast as islands, with stripes to rival lightning strikes.

The animals are fruitful and multiply. The paper zoo springs from her fingers. Banknotes flower and seed the carpet. Vegetation bends roots, branches and leaves for itself. New creatures flex their flesh and stretch their legs. The savannah, forest, jungle, tundra and desert expand into their own corners. Lumeina sits at the center of the world.

She forgot something.

Lumeina dashes to the bathroom. She floods the tub with sea and fills the depths with miniature sea monsters. Reefs bud and colonies creep along the porcelain pool. Lumeina wanders the waters with her hands. She smiles at the sight of familiar armor.

She reclines at the ocean's edge – leans against a mountainside. Her legs dangle over into a canyon, her toes dip into a river, the river meanders into forest, spills into jungle before trickling through savannah.

THOUSAND DOLLAR BUTTERFLY

96 A tornado overturns the savannah. It uproots baobabs and umbrella-thorns, sends them tumbling off like broccoli. Herds on the move are divided. The double-doors sweep aside the wildlife. The land shudders as a giant invades. Clouds fall from the sky. Clothes spill and landslide.

Jí-Min pins an elephant underfoot. He picks it off the floor – reads the banknote's value. It is an expensive elephant. He turns the animal inside-out.

He stoops and finds money trees, money flowers and weeds, five-hundred-dollar dinosaurs, millions worth all sprawled out upon the earth. He tramples the landscapes, reverses the artwork, quashes creation. He hunts for their maker.

A paper ship bobs in still bathwaters. Its body shelters dozens of animals – all poking their heads and hands from the top decks. Lumeina balances on the tub's edge with one leg in the ocean – the other a ramp rising off the tile. She guides more passengers aboard – a whole line of them await, winding around the bathroom floor and out the door.

Jí-Min stares with fists full of butchered origami. "What are you doing!"

Lumeina notices him at the doorway. He shoves the door into the wall. Cash spews like confetti. The bathwater ripples.

"Are you screwed up!" He stomps her creatures flat. "What did you make all these for! What good are they!" He mauls the small bodies into skins and hides. He glares at her. She shields the Ark behind her.

Jí-Min shoves her to the floor. He lifts the boat off the water and smashes it onto her. The bills scatter into beams of timber and piles of carcasses. They bury her in money.

He storms off – searches for the bags, finds a final sack full of yellow books. He dips his hand into the bag and brings a book to his face. Lumeina watches from the bathroom floor.

He glares at her and checks the bag for more. He flips through the book. The banknotes flutter in his hands – sweeping across his thumb. They begin to fold as they pass under his grip. They all spring into wings. Butterflies launch from the bundle and swipe at his face. He dodges them.

They pile at his feet – hundreds of thousands of dollars locked in an origami garden.

"Sèí Bot-Pàw! Unfold them now!" he shouts into the bathroom.

Lumeina is not there.

She stands over the money bag.

He grasps a butterfly and flattens it in his palms. The paper catches and slashes his hand. He drops the butterfly knife and snatches the bag. He rushes off but the sack erupts like a confetti cannon. Books of origami unsheathe. Reams of razor wings scourge his face. He staggers onto the paper traps, they shred his shoes – pierce his feet. He catches himself against the counter.

Lumeina approaches. The banknotes shuffle aside for her, bowing soft under her feet and flitting along her train. She inspects Jí-Min's open face, traces his split cheek and seals the wound. She writes along the scab: *Where is my dress?*

Jí-Min pauses at the sound of her voice. It sizzles through his spine like a branding iron. He gasps. The cuts on his face bleed like sweat. He sees his tattered face in her blacked eyes: "You can't wear the dress anymore. They'll recognize you..."

She asks again: *MY DRESS!*

"Fix – fix my face and I'll tell you," he stammers. He stares at himself.

Then at nothing. Her eyes blacken further. She rests her fingers on his eyes: *I will do better than fix – I will erase your face.* She mends the slits in his eyelids first.

She over-mends.

未完面

His eyelids stitch together and smooth out at the seams. He never had eyelids at all.

Jí-Min strains the muscles around his eyes. The lids twitch and struggle to separate. His eyeballs writhe under the flawless skin.

He screams at them to open.

Lumeina wipes his lips with her fingertips. Flesh closes over his mouth. His lips merge into a single mask. His own skin muzzles him. He never had lips at all.

Then his ears: the earlobes coil and withdraw into his head – like shy tubeworms. And then his nose: mucous clots and curdles up his nostrils, fills them in with flesh. He makes air holes for himself, picking his nose until it bleeds too much to breathe.

He never had a face.

He slumps into the bed of butterflies. He plays with the knives. They sink their wings into his body. They drink his warm red dye. He swims blind and drowns in the dark.

DEBUTANTE

97 The setting sun stains the windows orange. Everything in the suite rusts orange.

Crisp shopping bags wait by the double-doors. Origami herds parade Jí-Min's body into the bedroom and seal the mausoleum. Others parade the shopping bags to Lumeina's feet – parade like rustling autumn leaves. She sits with them, searches through the bags. She spreads out the jeans and tops.

The fresh clothes – she smells someone within their folds.

She presses the white hooded sweater to her nose – breathes in the woman's aroma. Her scent is laced with soap and fragrance. Lumeina inhales deeper. She finds Jí-Min entwined in the woman's scent. Then something else – a familiar dress.

She pulls the sweater over her head, fits into the cotton. She slips into the cargo pants, fastens the button.

Lumeina's face fades into the shade of her hood. Her long strands hang from the collar. A black mask eclipses her face.

Another outfit idles – a button shirt and jeans. She crouches to the sleeping clothes, strokes the shirt's breast and the pants' waist:

生

Two hair strands slink from her hood and embroider the words where she traced.

The clothes fill and rise before her like helium balloons. A sleeve reaches for her hand and leads her out the suite, to the elevator, down the hotel, into the street. Lumeina's zoo forms a convoy behind her. The paper creatures cascade down the stairwell. Some paraglide and others parachute from the high-rise windows. All process like a march of leaves in the jaws of leaf-cutter ants.

Hotel staff makes way. Evening traffic makes way. Pedestrians make way. No one stands in their way. Everyone stares at the invisible man leading the girl in boy clothes escorted by origami army.

WOLVES IN WOOL

98 The electric razor hovers like a hummingbird. Its beak slides over his scalp, wipes nectar from his pores, pecks off remaining stamen.

A white hose inhales his follicles from sight. The nurses brush stray hairs off his nape and brow. Their white masks hide Dr. Wòng from the dark. They begin to shave his face.

They pull the shaver along his cheek. They pull again – again, but the hair resists. The nurse checks the razor, unclips the unit. Fine black pepper puffs from the tool. The dust cloud smears the perfect white. Wòng eyes the stain.

The nurses eye Wòng's scalp and notice ingrown hairs weaving under and over his skin – like sidewinder snakes racing across the desert. The strands drape his head and drool down his face. The hairs lift his skin like a plastic film before piercing free.

The dust-seeds sprout black weeds. The nurses scrape the mold off their sleeves, rake the vacuum nozzle over the lawn – but vines crawl free and bind the barbers. Hair clippings climb out of the hose – the suction stretches them as they reach for Wòng. They emerge from their den.

"What do you want!" Wòng cries, "I did as you told!"

The emerging strands braid into a serpent's body. Dragon jaws protrude from the head. Fangs spray the room with acid. The lips purr at the doctor and the tongue frays. Wòng sweats squid ink.

The dragon grips Wòng, lays its face against his ear. Its tongue spears into his ear canal and drips into him: *But hate you did not. Your betrayal you regret. Never we forget, never we regret. Always we return...*

The vacuum groans as it vomits. Venom blinds all from the exit. The white room blacks out.

SCHEMESTRESS

99 The lights go off. Only a few bulbs keep night watch. The sales assistant locks her department, gathers her purse and bag. She walks the empty aisles.

She recognizes the hooded sweater.

But not the mannequin.

She checks the display – wades into the racks and stacks of clothes. She reaches for the sweater.

It reaches for her.

She leaps, but gloves grab her arms. She screams, but sleeves shut her face. A floating shirt wraps her – jeans bind her. She searches for the face in the hood – the face in silhouette, the face she does not see. She swings free, whips and aims a can of aerosol. She empties the pepper spray into the deep black blank.

The hood flutters. Long hairs flicker and fall to the floor. The hood turns to the assistant's bag. The black dress rises like a cobra before a charmer.

The hairs slither to the racks and stacks. The strands burrow into the fabrics – weaving throughout the threads, embracing the fibers. Possessed pants seek shirts and the shirts seek pants. Blouses seek skirts and skirts seek tops. Ties seek collars, shoes seek socks, gloves seek sleeves. Dresses hop from their hooks.

The assistant looks at the shop lifting itself to its feet.

She glances back.

A girl stands in the black dress.

The vacated sweater and cargo pants stand by. The shirt and jeans release the assistant. She watches the girl with the long hair lead the crowd of empty clothes. They leave the mall and join the night life.

Moon Festival

100 Lumeina follows the red lanterns. The paper balloons adorn the night sky like buoys in the sea. She walks the emptying street – everyone clearing away at the sight of her entourage. The clothes drape the streetlights and stoplights. They press to the road and buildings – flat and creeping like mantas. They darken the night, then set themselves alight with the lanterns.

A structure down the street brightens its windows. The glass drips colors into the night. Lumeina follows the glow. She reads the reds, blues and yellows. Every step closer tingles more and more. Music trickles through the air, up the pavement. The resonance tickles her feet.

She emerges alone from the dark street. She ascends the marble steps – cold and rippling under her feet. The teak doors muffle the music. Lumeina spots the words engraved on the archway:

大教堂夜總會

The stained windows flash like strobes and disco balls. The bell tower and spires fly red banners and flags. The buttresses twitch over the building like anxious fingers.

Men watch her approach. With their eyes they check her dress, touch her flesh. They run their sights through her hair. She stops and meets them at the summit of the steps.

"No clothes allowed."

She stands and looks at the doors. She steps forward.

They grab her straps: "No clothes!"

A lion pounces onto the steps – its body a mass of origami teeth and muscles, a wardrobe of fur and mane. The lion-puppet stares down security. It reddens its button eyes, smacks its zipper lips, bares its paper-saber fangs, flexes its retractable stiletto-heel claws. It mauls the marble steps into shards.

The men release Lumeina. They back away from the predator.

It advances.

They flee down the dark street.

It pursues.

All they hear behind them is the sound of laundry and banknotes shuffling in the wind – lots of laundry, and even more emerge from hiding. They merge into the beast, enlarging its prowess.

The silent lion dances after the men – prowls and seeks to devour.

ECSTASY AND ESCHATON

101 The unguarded doorway opens to Lumeina. She enters.

Inside, lanterns light the stalls along the walls. Each booth offers a woman locked in pillory, knelt behind latticework. Each anonymous body is posed behind a screen like a shadow puppet. Each pew nearby is heavy with men – each waiting to stand before a moist mouth.

The nave is crowded with men and stained red under a school of paper pufferfish. Altars at each column twinkle with cold chalices, sweaty wine glasses and sweaty women chained to statues.

Younger women lay shackled on the main altar – their bodies blanketed with a banquet. Men pick meat, fish, shrimp, fruit and mooncakes from their flesh. Chopsticks poke the girls, hands stroke the girls, lips lick the girls – but the girls laze and blink their wet eyes.

Lumeina hears only their hearts. Many gush with lust. Others throb with daggers in their chambers. Some sob as beggars among strangers. The music masks their prayers.

She cuts to the chancel – through the writhing horde. Her hair machetes men on contact. The music masks their screams.

The music stops.

The disc jockey smacks the dance floor face first. Eyes trace his fall from the choir loft.

Agent Lau fills the silence – his words boom over the speakers: "Behold the holy sacrifice of the masses... the Cathedral of the Party welcomes you! Little Miss Chúng..." His voice deepens from hyena howl to gorilla growl.

Gunfire erupts.

Soldiers storm the sanctuary. They gun down everyone to gun down Lumeina.

She stands her ground. She enjoys the show of empty costumes.

Pants lasso and noose. Shirts embalm. Skirts smother and blouses suffocate. Ties garrote, shoes and boots bludgeon, gloves strangle, and dresses bag bodies.

Bullets poke dots into the skirts, breathing-holes into the body bags. Blood patterns the outfits with paisley.

Her origami army flurries in – swells the doorways and airways. The papers cut open weapons, armor and people. They slash, they bite, they maul and gnaw. They stab, pierce, gore and slaughter. They cover bodies like flies on carrion, like maggots on decay. They adorn the dead like fungus.

Candles and lanterns set the forest of corpses on fire. The dresses go kamikaze and fit their trains with flames. They embrace the men and chase to no end.

Her hair lengthens, blackens. Her eyes darken. She grins and her teeth bleed black blood. The paper locusts mate with the flames and shrill like cicadas. They spawn ash.

"AH-FEI!"

Lumeina hears his heart skip.

All noise ends.

He slumps to the floor – his body slaps the tile. All papers slap the tile. All empty clothes slap the tile. She turns to him at the foot of the aisle. She runs to him – her feet slap the tile. She stoops. Her knees slap the tile. His blood laps the tile. A red carpet blooms around the couple. The fires sear his wandering blood.

She trembles in his puddle. She lifts his head from the red, rests him on her legs. His hair brushes her belly. Her breath is quick and shudders. His breath is slow and stutters. Her skin and eyes drip hot. His skin and eyes do not.

She caresses his body with her fingers – writes his name everywhere. She plucks the paper wings lodged in his wounds. She rubs the gashes – begs them to shut and mend, but they stare at her, their eyes wide and scowling. They drool at her – spit at her.

She buries her face into his hair, inhales the grime. He cools. Her hair slopes into his puddle. Her sweat and tears dilute his red. Her fingers fumble and scribble on his bleeding body, her waters wash words into the blood – but nothing legible.

He whispers through his lips – through his flogged flesh and bones, "Fei... take this..." He tugs the salt pouch from his pocket. He fumbles and the crystals tinkle: "I kept it – for you." Loose snowflakes season and bless his wounds.

She nods and trembles – holds the salt to her breast, slides it to the back pocket on her dress.

"Luu... I'm sorry I... left you. I'm not afraid-lah – not afraid..."

Then don't leave me... not again...

"I'm not – it only looks... that way. I'm staying... not leaving-lah. Don't be afraid..."

Ah-Yíng...

He smiles: "You look... just like your mother."

Lumeina gazes upon his face. She reads his eyes – he locks onto her collar, follows her star scars. She places her hand on the cicatrix – it leads her fingers to the medal. She takes Yíng's hand and presses it to the woman. They hold her together.

She hears his song echo, feels his blood slow... trickle... cease. The light in his eyes darkens.

SMARTER FARTER

102 Laughter spews from the organ pipes. The wide throats bellow – the thin bleat. The choir buffets the chamber with hyena, chimpanzee, walrus and gorilla. Each pipe gives voice to each mouth in Lau's gut. A mob mocks Lumeina.

She rises. Loose strands lift from her hair. The slim serpents swim the wind up to the agent. They snatch him from the choir loft and bring him to her.

She glares at him.

He glares back – his eyes as absent as hers.

The hair on her head fans into a black peacock plume. The array clamps onto her, binds her face in a helmet. She snatches the strands, claws and tears at the bindings. The hair chains and contains her. The helmet wrings her head. She collapses – struggles.

The cowl parts around her eyes. It forms a telescope over each eyeball. Her eyelashes pin her eyes open and into place. Lau force-feeds Lumeina:

Yíng rises off the floor – Lau peels his body from the red paste. Her lover's blood cries out to her from the ground. Lau turns Yíng to face her, raises the young man's finger against her, fills the corpse's lungs with laughter, shapes the face into wrath: "You killed me! Fei! Scary Fei! SCARY FEI!" His jaws chomp like a nutcracker.

Yíng's wounds grin her way. His bared bones glisten like teeth and his torn flesh pucker like lips. They woo her: "Luu, Luu, Luu, Luu, Luu, Luu, Luu, Luu..."

Lau embraces Yíng from behind – melts into the young body. His parasites sift into the fresh host. The open wounds salivate as Yíng's corpse approaches her, touches her, kisses her with his hundred lips. They suckle her pores.

The corpse's jugular writhes and clenches its vocal cords. The hundred lips sputter against her skin: "You smell sweeeet... Fei... forgive me for I have sinnned. It has been never since my last confession. Here is my sinnn: I desired to rape you and your mother while you were within her... I still desire..."

Lumeina vomits.

The zombie rubs her belly and sips her spit. It bites her lips and whispers down her throat, "You deserve better do you think? Forgiveness and love you deserve?" It grips Lumeina's face through the helmet. It peels her from its hungry lips, dangles her by her face. It stares into her the whole time.

"Betrayed you have been. Utterly deceived! By your lover. By your mother!" The corpse closes its hands around her head and crushes. "Familiar is this? The stress, the pressing, the crushing... your very murder your own mother sought!" Its hands meld into her. "Loved you were not. Loved you will never be!"

The pulse in her skull throbs and pangs. Lumeina kicks off from the body. It catches her feet in its flesh. Its open sores bleed black. The blood separates into threads. Nose hairs crawl forth like spider legs. The hairs fix Lumeina onto the corpse. It snags her like a sundew.

The corpse positions her and widens its mouth. Its face separates into blooming Venus flytrap lips. The darkness behind its teeth deepens.

"To us you belong. Your only true desirers we are." Its fangs fondle her neck.

The corpse twists her around, presses her low – her back to its howling navel. Its bellybutton bites her like a toothless mouth. It casts her forward, throws her head into kowtow. It crouches low behind her and aims. Ingrown hairs curl from its skin and join the consummation. The hairs burrow through the pants and preen her surface.

She aims – supper gas erupts from deep within her tunnels. Her butt burp holds off the assault, kicks back her skirt, thrusts the salt pouch out her pocket. The crystals scald and blister the corpse's crotch – routing its hairs off her. The zombie's seed spills and screams upon the salt. Its rotten fruits wither off their stem.

The corpse shrieks and stumbles away. The diamond dust lands near its feet. It does not touch it.

The corpse stomps Lumeina into the floor – stomps her unconscious: "Anathema! Unclean! Unworthy! Unlovable! Unredeemable! Unforgivable!"

It hauls her to the main altar, slams her atop the dead. It mounts. Dishes scatter and warp under their weight. Berries, oranges, pineapple, mango, kiwi – they rot on contact. The kiwi peel itches her skin before it decays – itches of sackcloth.

The corpse whispers decay into her: "You dare to return? to reach? when Hell is your just home? You dare believe you can be made new? Vile lies! You are the First Fallen – Forever Fallen."

Lumeina's black dress decays along. Its plush touch blemishes and browns – crisps and crusts like roasted peanut husks.

FLUTTERFLY

103 The black butterfly descends on Lumeina. Its wings shed its stars upon her. It knights her with its flitting black blades – ignites her with its gaze.

The corpse grabs the butterfly off her hair. It closes its fist around the wings. The insect bursts into sun-dust. Flares and coronas orbit its grip.

A blade of light beams through the zombie's knuckles – severs its fingers. Coils of leeches spill from the amputation. They squeal and slobber to the floor. The fingers smolder like joss sticks.

Another blade shears through the corpse's wrist. Four more unfold. The six wings burn the hand off the arm. White fire chases up the limb, gnaws into its chest.

Black maggots leak out the corpse's throat. They stare at the light forcing themselves off Lumeina. The rays separate them from her. They withdraw from the heat.

Twin worms slither out the corpse's nostrils like a nosebleed. They extend and twine into a mustache: "Begone! Unjust you are... Behold! These many millennia she refused to serve, to obey. Leave us with her! One of us she is. With her we fell – with us she remains. Just we are!"

The light glares into them. It focuses on the parasites: "Asmodeus-Abaddon – we meet again."

The worms fatten. They bulge out the nose, bloat the face, burst the skull like a rotten squash. They hiss in unison:

Ráphaël

The Archangel beats the salt pack into the corpse's gaping face. The body regurgitates as the sacramental corrodes the corruption.

The vipers throw the body to the floor, drag it to the door. The cremains jitter like maracas. Centipedes and millipedes unravel from the crumbling den. The plague screeches off.

The Archangel launches and strikes them into slivers. The salt erupts into jewels and gems. The marble floor melts and freezes into lightning-glass. The fulgurite floor ignites the prowlers and crawlers.

They dissolve like lit fuses.

THE FALL

104 Lumeina lies on her side and watches from atop the altar – her legs tucked to her chest, her arms holding them close. The walking lightning grazes over the marble floor – searing every tile it touches into diamond. She fills her eyes with its light.

She follows the light as it rises to the stained windows. The colored crystals soften, grow fluid and flow. The glass dances and the windows animate. She follows the moving pictures from window to window – follows as they loop the sanctuary walls. They glow and show Lumeina the beautiful WOMAN – crowned with Heaven and robed with the sun. Her halo and its gems blush all the angels. They sit at her feet and gather near her womb. They lean their ears to her flesh and hear the song of two hearts.

Heaven adores.

All of Heaven but one.

A great light below her feet begins to seethe. Its fumes stain Heaven. Its smoke soils its sibling lights – singes faces and stings eyes. It tempts others to betray.

The WOMAN embraces her belly. She guards her child from the rising smoke.

The fumes darken and fester. It burns the WOMAN's tears into steam. The black smoke spreads and screams:

non serviam!

It buries the sky.

But then, little lightning cleaves the smoke into fragments. The bolts burst from a small flicker – a mere lightning bug in the smoldering dust storm.

Yet its lightning impales the fumes. It thunders as it thrusts. Its mighty shield guards the QUEEN and its battle cry challenges the storm's might:

quis ut deus?!

Other cries join in and the choir expands – reclaims. The lightning storm binds the smoke. The fumes slump under the tears of the VIRGIN. Her bitter rain blisters the floor of Heaven.

The sky falls.

And the seethers fall with it.

They fall together – crackling down the night sky like cinders. The lightning dashes them to the earth in chains – burning the black into blue and the blue into black. The sky sizzles and scars. The winds and clouds char. The stars above remain and the stars below snuff out.

They strike the sea. They burn a hole into the ocean. The earth bleeds and bruises.

A leech slithers from the bruise. It bores along the land and sniffs footprints. It tracks the feet – smears the prints into claws, into feet with long spikes driven through them.

The feet lead to a flowerbed within a garden. A man leaps from sleep, kneels beside his bride. His body blushes, his blood trills and his heart hears his beloved's – and her heart hears hers. They listen to each other. They listen together.

The woman rises from her bouquet bed. She sits, smiles and laughs while her groom's body dances to her song. The bridegroom and bride dance the day away to their song.

Their dance wanders throughout the garden. They wander past a tree with two high branches and a proud trunk. Its sap drools down its body and penetrates the earth. The man gazes up the tree and reads its leaves fanning the breeze. The sun dusts the sifting leaves – lets him see into the tree's lush crown. A brother sleeps within the hanging garden – tucked upon a bed of wood.

Smoke rises up to the brother. The man watches the wind darken. The dark wind unsheathes its talons, strips the tree naked, scourges its tender bark, gnaws its core for thick sap. Leaves fall to the ground like singed skin.

The brother is taken from his bed and pinned to the tree's spine. The wind claws his dripping face with a kiss.

The wind sears his breaths with cinder. The wind wrings his flesh for sweat – wrings for blood and water.

The man watches the wind pluck and juice the brother. The tree's proud trunk sags with sap even thicker – even richer. Its roots flow as rivers red with warmth. The earth drinks.

The wind casts off the brother – swift gusts consume his body. The tree returns to new life.

The dark wind falls from the tree onto the man, surrounds him and threatens. It pecks his ears and prods his song.

He stops singing.

He steps aside.

The smoke proceeds to his bride, it softens and runs through the woman's hair. It wraps her with whispers – asks her to stare, to doubt and to want. She peers into the new leaves and the new fruits. She reaches for their great height and the wind lowers the branches – presses the tree's arms to her feet.

The wind woos her with its decadent song and leprous caresses.

The tree bleeds white.

The woman tastes the tree's unripe seed. Lonesomeness fills her appetite. The seed's bitter blood stains her black. She shares with the man and he watches the black blood. He remembers the dark wind – threatening... threatening.

He takes.

Doubt feeds the man's stomach with hunger – the woman's womb with sorrow. The dark wind laughs at the man and woman.

The man's body pulses against his will. The woman's body bleeds against her.

The dark wind rains leeches onto the man and woman. The black worms lather their naked bodies in black sputum. The long thin maggots swell and plump as they burrow the couple's stale flesh – lacing the woman's heart with chains and the man's strength with tyranny. The smoke blackens into squid ink and climbs into their mouths – chews through their teeth and claws down their throats. It mines them and plants mines deep in their bones.

Black rain stains the gift. All around the man and woman, flowers burn brown, leaves pepper the air with their ashes, waters drown their fish, and lands starve their animals. The song ends and wailing begins.

The man and woman do not hold each other. His sweat burns her flesh and her touch accuses his skin – like lightning blistering clouds and piercing sky. He stares at her body and will not see her face. She hides from his stares because of his face. She hides under dead leaves and he hides with her.

The sun searches for them – longs for the man and woman. The light walks and finds the man and woman hidden beneath black festers and tinder. They look away. The sun's gaze shames their flesh. Their bodies lose their luster.

The woman looks to the man and weeps in the light. The man raises his finger to the light and points another to the woman. His finger draws her tears.

The woman finds a leech suckling her. She sheds the plump worm and flings it to her heel. She points down to Lumeina – her fingertip poised between Lumeina's eyes, trapped in Lumeina's stare.

The stained windows freeze in place. The colors stiffen and the frames cease their dance.

The final frame hardens, then fractures around the woman's hand. A long mangled fingernail protrudes.

THE EXORCESS

105 Lumeina's pupils dilate into solid obsidian. Her black hair flickers. Her flesh bleaches powder white and her tears bleed black. Each droplet sprouts legs and scampers back into her – burrowing into her pores, wounds, and openings. Her porcelain body reveals her every vein and artery – darkening, hardening like glazed china, binding her from within.

Her pupils retreat and her hair rests. Her milk and honey complexion returns richer than before. They soothe her – sweeten her.

Her hair twitches and her eyes tremble. Her head quivers and her body shivers. She grits her teeth until they fracture.

They shush her – seek to pleasure. They flower black strawberries from the ends of her hair. They feed her and touch her, stimulate and massage everywhere.

Lumeina spits them out.

She twists her hands into her hair and rips them out. She weeds and uproots her scalp, peels it like ripe rambutan. The growth bleeds on her fingernails, clings like black lichen, splits her nails into splinters.

The hair writhes in her fists. It gnaws through her palms, exits through her wrists. They pounce to her feet, sink their teeth. The strands encase her arms and legs like sausage meat, reattaching like lampreys and leeches. They snare her like a net, cling like cobwebs, nip her with their split ends.

The cathedral is silent but for the sound of peeling oranges.

The hairs thresh her flesh: *Rid us you cannot! Hell your home is. Hell you are...*

Lumeina kicks and curls. The man drags her about the altar top. She presses the hair onto her cicatrix. They squea and toast into brimstone incense.

Her grip slicks with sweat and blood. The hair slips free. She latches onto the altar, slams her head to the stone – beats the hair caught between marble and bone. She bludgeons her skull and weeps at the finger pointing from the window. It accuses her: *You killed us! Fei! Scary Fei!*

The marble crumbles.

She crumbles into the crumbs.

The hair tires – weighed down by dewdrops caught in its strands. It flops in the slop.

A dewdrop moistens her lips.

Lumeina touches the strawberry blood with her tongue – traces its path to the ceiling. The mangled man hangs from crossed beams – His feet trickle sap tapped from His head, hands and side. His sweat ferments the juice into wine, the wine into blood.

She watches blood and water rain. He bleeds into her.

Soft hands cradle her broken head. Fingers wipe her face with burlap sleeves. She feels a warm bosom against her cheek. Roses sweeten the air. Lumeina nibbles the breath with her lips.

The beautiful woman gazes down on her. The altar is her lap and arms. She holds Lumeina.

Seven swords are lodged in the woman's breast – the blades twitch with her every pulse. The man on the cross and the woman's hearts hum together. Lumeina hears him above – hears him within:

múlier ecce fília tua...

fília ecce mater tua...

Lumeina touches a blade – warm in her fingers. Her stained hands taint the crystal. The woman smiles. She brushes Lumeina's hair and Legion slops off to the floor – limp and languid as cold noodles. In their place are bright black gossamers tipped with stars.

The tangled mop sloughs off – slinks to the corner and

Lumeina presses her fingers to the woman's chest – into the space between the blades. The woman's heart is hot and throbbing. Lumeina strokes with her fingertips:

阿媽...

Her hand falls – pale, cold and open.

Mother catches her falling hand. She lifts it to her lips and nods, "Shhh... shhhh... I know – I know..." She rests her fingers over the girl's slowing heart:

阿女...

Mother's words course into her broken ivory body. She drinks it in like warm milk.

Columns of light gather around the mother and daughter. Their light bleaches the stained windows. Their light rounds the altar, lines the pews, aisles, confessionals, loft and nave. Two columns ascend the steps and kneel beside the woman and child.

"Ah-Neõi..."

"Ah-Fei..."

Lumeina turns to them. They rest their hands on her.

"Come home with us..."

"Everyone's waiting for you..."

Lumeina watches the light fade. The altar is damp beneath her body. The cathedral is hazy with dust floating in sunrise. The stained windows tint the fog.

She is alone.

She rests her eyes upon the brightest window – the sun just on the other side. The fractures heal into a smooth pane. The hand in the final frame accuses no more. It waits for her with an open hand.

Lumeina looks up to the open hand, up the arm onto the shoulders of the Mother – and from the Mother to the Son. They both bow to the Father and their daylight bathes Lumeina in song. Their light breathes and its breath touches her. Everything glows gold in its touch: the tips of her hair, the wrinkles in her gown, the cracks in the wall, the dust in the air, the wounds in her. She remembers young summer breezes in the garden. Her tousled hair leans back and into place, her face brightens but she only looks at the gaze – her eyes wide, her lips sometimes touching and sometimes not, and her body unmoving. She is still for many moments.

Moments pass.

She dips her head – nods without turning her eyes away. The gaze does not dissolve, the warmth remains, the summer persists, the bath freshens. She nods and nods and whispers, "Yes... yes..." – unable to hear anything but shouts and new song.

"SHE WHO WAS NOT BELOVED
I SHALL CALL 'MY BELOVED.'"

ROMANS 9:25

GLOSSARY OF GREGORIAN CHANT AND LATIN TERMS

(By chapter of first appearance)

Gregorian Chant (aka: plain chant) is an ancient form of sung Christian prayer originating from the era of Pope St. Gregory the Great in the Seventh Century.

Latin	Ch.	English
salve regina, mater misericórdiæ, vita, dulcédo, et spes nostra salve...	5	Hail, Holy Queen, Mother of Mercy, our life, our sweetness and our hope...
philomena	8	"Child of Light"
ego te baptízo in nómine patris et fílii et spíritus sancti.	8	"I baptize you in the name of the Father and of the Son and of the Holy Spirit." –Matthew 28:19
miserére mei, deus... secúndum magnam misericórdiam tuam...	20	Have mercy on me, God... according to Your great kindness...
serenus	31	Serene, tranquil, peaceful
azarias	32	Hebrew for: "Help of God." –Tobias/Tobit 5:18
venenum	46	Venom, poison
ave maría, grátia plena, dóminus tecum, benedícta tu in muliéribus et benedíctus fructus ventris tui, iesus...	50	Hail Mary, full of grace, the Lord is with thee, Blessed art thou among women and blessed is the fruit of thy womb, Jesus... –Luke 1:28
pater noster, qui es in cælis, sanctificétur nomen tuum, advéniat regnum tuum, fiat volúntas tua sicut in cælo et in terra...	51	Our Father, who art in Heaven, hallowed be Thy name, Thy kingdom come, Thy will be done on Earth as it is in Heaven... –Matthew 6:9-13
rorate cæli désuper – et nubes pluant justum...	78	Drop down dew, ye heavens, from above, and let the clouds rain the just...
stabat mater dolorósa, juxta crucem lacrymósa, dum pendébat fílius. cujus ánimam geméntem contristátem et doléntem, pertransívit gládius. o quam tristis et afflícta, fuit illa benedícta, mater unigéniti...	83	At the Cross her station keeping, Stood the mournful Mother weeping, Close to her Son to the last. Through her heart, His sorrow sharing, All His bitter anguish bearing, Now at length the sword has passed. O how sad and sore distressed Was that Mother, highly blest, Of the sole-begotten One.
duc in altum	84	"Put out into the deep." –Luke 5:4
ráphaël	103	Hebrew for: "God heals." –Tobias/Tobit 5:4
non servíam!	104	"I will not serve!"
quis ut deus?!	104	"Who is like God?" –Revelation 12
múlier ecce fília tua... fília ecce mater tua...	105	"Woman, behold, thy daughter... Daughter, behold, thy Mother...." –John 19: 26-27

GLOSSARY OF CHINESE TERMS
(By chapter of first appearance)
Cantonese pronunciation marks are only approximate.

= = =

路西法	*Lòw-Sèi-Fot* = Lucifer, Latin for: "Light Bearer"
小姐	*Sèéw-Jèèh* = Little Miss; Miss; young lady
菲洛梅娜	[8] *Fei-Luò-Méi-Nà* = Philomena, Latin for: "Child of Light"
耶穌	[9] *Yèh-Sóh* = Yeshua, Aramaic for: "Jesus"
阿	[13] *"Ah-"* = (prefix attached to noun to show affection)
女	[13] *Neōi* = daughter; girl; feminine; female
媽	[13] *Máh* = mother, mom, mommy
哎吔 / 哎呀	[15] *Ai-yah* = "Oh my goodness!" (common interjection)
快快	[15] *Fai-Fai* = quick-quick (repeated for emphasis)
你會死	[16] *Nàý Wooý Sèi* = "You will die."
殞	[16] *Wáhn* = to perish, to vanish
受苦	[16] *Sàu Fóó* = to suffer bitterly
炮烙	[16] *Pao Lawk* = tortured and seared to death with a molten pillar
插針	[16] *Chop Júm* = tortured and pierced to death with needles
罹難	[16] *Lèi Nàn* = to die disastrously
慘死	[16] *Chōm Sèi* = to die tragically
瑪利亞	[19] *Ma-Lèi-Áh* = Miriam, Hebrew for: "Maria", "Mary"
冇	[24] *Mōh* = stop, cease, do not; have not
聖經	[24] *Sing-Ging* = Holy Scripture, Bible
爸	[30] *Bàh* = father, dad, daddy
范英	[33] *Fàn-Yíng* = Fàn (a Chinese surname), Yíng (victor, hero)
圖書館	[34] *Tòw Seé Góón* = library
教堂	[34] *Gau Tòng* = church; chapel
十	[34] *Sùp* = ten, one more than nine, one less than eleven

243

大	[36] *Dài* = large, big; elder, older
慢慢來	[38] *Màhn-Màahn Lèi* = "Take your time"
咩	[40] *Mèh* = "What?", "Huh?"
安娜	[43] *Ah-Nàh* = Hannah, Hebrew for: "Anne", "Anna"
走	[51] *Jàú* = to scat, leave, flee, run
吁瑪利亞,	*Oh Mary,*
無原罪之始胎,	*Conceived without sin,*
我等奔爾臺前,	*Pray for us,*
為我等祈.	*Who have recourse to Thee.*
喂	[55] *Wey/Wai* = "Hey!" (common slang greeting)
未完面	[55] *Mèi-Yeùn-Meèn* = "Not Yet-Finished-Face"
斃	[70] *Bài* = die, meet execution, perish
死	[73] *Séi* = to die, dead, death (may be used as a curse)
大陸仔	[73] *Dài-Loòk-Jéi* = "Mainland Boy" (derogatory)
彌額爾	[77] "Michael", Hebrew for: "Who is like God?"
味精	[80] *Mèi Jíng* = monosodium glutamate (MSG)
她是個秘密	[80] "She is a secret."
屎	[81] *Sèé* = feces, excrement, shit (slang)
伯	[82] *Baak* = uncle (respectful way to address elderly men)
雞	[87] *Géi* = chicken, hen, chick; prostitute (derogatory)
來	[91] *Lèi* = "come along"
死八婆	[96] *Sèi Bot-Pàw* = "Dead-Bitch"
生	[97] *Sàhng* = live, raw, alive
大教堂夜總會	[100] "Cathedral Night Club"

= = =

MORE INFORMATION REGARDING CANTONESE-CHINESE AVAILABLE AT:
WWW.CANTONESE.SHEIK.CO.UK
AND REGARDING CHINESE LANGUAGE IN GENERAL:
WWW.NCIKU.COM

GLOSSARY OF COMMON CANTONESE-CHINESE FINAL PARTICLES

(In no particular order)

Cantonese-Chinese suffixes (particles) express
emphasis, emotion, exaggeration, etc.
when linked to the end of words, phrases, sentences.

= = =

呀	-ah	Varied uses. Tonal changes in pronouncement alters meaning to express: tenderness, accusation, anger, patience, even apathy.
嗎	-mah	Changes the host word or phrase into a question.
喎	-waw	Expresses concern, worry, goodwill.
囉	-loh	Adds an element of nostalgia or importance because of past events.
咩	-méh	Used in or as a question expressing surprise or disbelief.
啦	-lah	Expresses satisfaction, completion, contentment, earnestness, or: impatience, frustration, annoyance.
㗎	-gah	Expresses anger or frustration, awe or amazement.
呢	-néh	Used to continue questions from previous remarks, or repeats the question but for a different subject. Also used for rhetorical questions.
啫	-jeh	De-emphasizes the word or statement. Also used as: "only" or "merely" or "that's all" - "It's only raining, that's all."
嘅	-guh	Adds a sense of possessiveness, or a reserved assertiveness.
嘅	-geh?	Emphasizes puzzlement, curiosity (pronounced as a question).

= = =

MORE INFORMATION REGARDING CANTONESE FINAL PARTICLES AT:
WWW.CANTONESE.SHEIK.CO.UK/ESSAYS/CANTONESE_PARTICLES.HTM

THE SECRET DAUGHTER
(Spoiler Alert!)

Ah-Neõi...

You are still too young to hear this, still too young to understand. Ah-Máh is writing this for your future, when you are ready to know, and in case Ah-Máh is unable to tell you... although Ah-Máh very much hopes to tell you everything in person.

Let Ah-Máh tell you more about the spirit – great and bright like the moon... shining, warm and singing:

When the spirit asked me if I would be your mother, of course I was frightened, but the spirit told me to not be afraid, that I was free to choose, that I would be loved by Ah-Bàh no matter what decision I made.

It was then that I asked the spirit for its name and he told me he was Gabriel the Archangel. It was then that I prayed to our Queen to help me – and since then I prayed so much that she would let you meet her one day... she is beautiful, more than anyone.

I listened to the angel carefully and then asked how this would happen to me, since all children need a mother and a father who love each other enough to give their love a name and a home, and because I did not have a husband to help me. I wanted to know what Ah-Bàh's will was.

The angel showed me. At first, I did not understand what I saw and could only wonder to myself, keeping it in my heart, but these years since I have more and more recognized what I was shown.

Ah-Neõi, you are special. Many parents believe this about their children, and what they believe is true, but you are not like other children. Your life did not begin when I became your mother, your life is much more ancient, and much more full of struggle.

I am yours – your mother. You are mine – my daughter. But I am not your only mother, and you are a daughter who has been missed for a very long time.

Once when I was little, my Mother Ah-Nàh was teaching me about the fallen angels: who they are, where they are from, and what made them so evil and ugly. I asked:

"If Ah-Bàh is so powerful and good, why doesn't he stop the evil angels? Why doesn't he throw them away?"

Mother Ah-Nàh told me something I would never forget. She said, "Because Ah-Bàh loves them too much to throw them away. He loves everything – all his creatures, forever. Ah-Bàh wants us all to be free to choose to love or to hate, because if we were forced to love, then it wouldn't be true. And he also knows some of us will choose to hate, but he took the risk. Ah-Bàh doesn't throw the bad creatures away because he wants his creatures to have the chance to change their minds, their hearts."

"Why? What's the reason love is so important?" I asked. Mother Ah-Nàh surprised me again:

"There is no reason for love because love is the reason. It's why Ah-Bàh made us and the angels and everything – so that he could love us and so that we could love Ah-Bàh and each other..."

Ah-Neõi, that is why Ah-Bàh did not throw you away. That is why you were created, and then born – to give you a chance to change your mind and heart... to choose to love.

I do not know how much you know about yourself, about your past before you were made into my daughter, before I was made into your mother, but I know Ah-Bàh will not keep your secret from you forever. Ah-Bàh will tell you everything, much more than Ah-Máh can, much better than Ah-Máh can – but only when Ah-Bàh decides it is your hour to know.

And when you discover yourself, please do not be ashamed... for I am not ashamed of being your mother, and Ah-Bàh is not ashamed of being your father. Do not let the truth shame you, but let the truth free you. Please trust and let it be...

I have prayed and keep praying for you – for our Queen to be with you always, and for her to send you a friend, a guardian and guide.

Ah-Neõi... Ah-Máh loves you. Remember that for yourself.

HEAR HER:

[MUSICAL INSPIRATIONS]
(In order of first appearance)
The following musical works guided or inspired the creation of
LITTLE MISS LUCIFER and have been adopted as the novel's own soundtrack:

= = =

"Affairs of the Heart" – MARJAN MOZETICH
"Salve Regina" (chant)
"Miserére Mei Deus" (chant)
"Ave María" (chant)
"Thunderstorm" – SOUNDS OF NATURE (live/recordings)
"ルージュ [Ru-Ju]" – MIYUKI NAKAJIMA (instrumental)
"Solo Whale" – SONGS OF THE HUMPBACK WHALE
"Stabat Mater Dolorósa" (chant)
"容易受傷的女人" – 王菲 [WÒNG, FAYE] (cover)
"Humphrey Clucas Crucifixus" – LAUDIBUS
"Crucifixus a 8" – ANTONIO LOTTI
"Veni Creátor Spíritus" (chant)

--- GENUINE GREGORIAN CHANT RECORDINGS BY "CANTORES IN ECCLESIA" AVAILABLE ON AMAZON.COM + iTUNES ---

LEARN ABOUT HER:

[EXORCISM AND DEMONOLOGY]
For information, personal accounts, and Church teaching regarding
the ancient Rite of Exorcism, please consider these resources:

= = =

FATHER GABRIELE AMORTH'S:
"An Exorcist Tells His Story"
"An Exorcist: More Stories"

= = =

FATHER JOSÉ ANTONIO FORTEA'S:
"Interview with an Exorcist"

= = =

MATT BAGLIO'S:
"The Rite: The Making of a Modern Exorcist"

= = =

www.FishEaters.com

ACKNOWLEDGEMENTS & CREDITS

(In no particular order)

Evan is grateful for these persons and prays for their well-being.
He also asks forgiveness for any errors that may be present.

= = =

INCREDIBLE INSPIRATIONS: The Father, Son and Spirit, Holy Mother Church, Sacred Scripture,
Archbishop Fulton J. Sheen, Flannery O'Connor, Saint Philomena,
Saint Joseph - the Terror of Demons, Saint Thérèse de Lisieux,
Saint Joan of Arc, Saint Thomas Aquinas, Saint Ignatius of Loyola,
Saint Augustine, Saint Louis-Marie de Monfort, Saint Teresa of Avila,
Saints Michael, Raphael, Gabriel the Archangels, & the Blessed Virgin Mary
-

ESSENTIAL EDUCATORS: ---Elementary School:
Mrs. Armstrong, Sara Bailey, Alice Girdler, Kathleen Kunnath, Judith LeBeau,
Mr. Snyder, Mr. Stogdill, Kathleen Swaney, Mrs. Grady, Mrs. Wilcox, Joanna
Woods, Mary Welsh, Marjorie Williams

---Middle School:
Robert Antczak, Ilene Arnold, Michelle Cooper, Henry Bielawski, David Craft,
Robert Dolinar, Laura Gorrill, Micki Kaminski, Terry Herron, Rick Jones,
Bonnie Linklater, Diane Malczyk, Frank Marberg, Evelyn Mazzola,
Donald Platter, Joe Strecansky, Christine Teper, Janis Trakul,
Michael Volchko, Diane Walerski

---High School:
Emily Brenner, Mark Kerpet, Chrystyna Kozak, J. Kus, Floyd Larson,
Bill McParlan, Gloria Schade, Marion Zehe
---Beverly Bartlett, Mrs. Benczik, Jennifer Boggio, Lee Bosma, Tim
Bussineau, Lisa Churilla, Jeanette Douglas, Shelley Dunkle, Karen Gardner,
Margaret Johnson, Scott Kim Lamb, Dave Lohr, John Palmateer,
Andrew Pyper, Laura Rienas, Christine Rowley, Erwin Slava,
Marianne Srock, Glenn Walters, Ralph Wiktor

---College:
Getnet Bekele, Linda Benson, Judith K. Brown, Gladys Cardiff,
Hsiang-Hua Chang, Jeff Chapman, Natalie B. Cole, Brian A. Connery,
Alan Epstein, Qian Gao, Rebecca Gaydos, Annette M. Gilson,
Edward Haworth Hoeppner, Linda McCloskey, Qiong Mei, Dawn Newton,
Jennifer G. Nguyen, Kathleen A. Pfeiffer, Doris Plantus, Mark Rigstad,
Samuel Rosenthall, Richard Stamps, Michelle Mei Tang, Pat Trentacoste,
Carol I. Trupiano, Sherry L. Wynn, Joshua Yumibe

Essential Educators
Continued:

---Catechism:
Deacon Francis Xavier Doan Chau, Huynh Thuc, Peter Nguyen Chi Nghia

---Vietnamese:
Huynh Ngoc Xuong, Le Hong Lan, Le Van Hiep, Pham Dung, Pham Huu Tung,
Tran Quoc Tuyen, Tran Thi Anh Tuyet

---and All Substitute Teachers involved in Evan's education.
-

Very Special Thanks to:
Yumi Ayrault, Olivia Blomquist, Ngan Bui, Maggie Chung, Natalie Clevenger,
Brian Connery, Maiko Connors, Huy-Linh & Rolaine Dang, Rose Demates,
Gloria Denomme, Nguyen Do, Erica Jeszke, Khoa Le, Kim & Teresa Le, Vy Le,
Alexander Nguyen, Jennifer Nguyen, Maria Hien Nguyen, Nghiem Nguyen,
Quynh Nguyen, Andrew Pham, Angela Pham, Doris Plantus, Jasmeet Singh,
Miho Sweeney, Maria Swenson, Team-Evan [straight from Heaven] (DHHS),
Team-Jeremiah (Sinai XIX), TNTT-USA, Jacob Tran, Julie Trieu, Angel Vo,
Davin Vo, Thien Vo, Timothy Vu, and Andrew Zoratti

---Our Lady of Grace Vietnamese Catholic Parish for being Evan's home and
church, and DATAD: VEYS/TNTT-Detroit for being Evan's youth group.

---and Thank You to the anonymous artists of the Marian Emblem gracing
the Dedication Page, and of the Invisible Blessed Virgin Mary Sculpture that
inspired the custom Chinese Miraculous Medal design in "Palisades".
-

Greatly Grateful for:
Popes John Paul the Great, Benedict XVI, and Francis,
Father Gabriele Amorth, Father Jose Antonio Fortea, Father Robert Barron,
Father Dennis Brown, Father Francis Budovic, Father Valentine Gattari,
Father Lam Chi Hoang, Father Tat-Thang Hoang, Father Benjamin Kosnac,
Father John Luong, Father Binh Nguyen, Father Vincent Nguyen,
Father Jeremy Paulin, Father John Riccardo, Father Francis Vu Tran,
Father Joseph Vu Duc, and all Holy Priests and Consecrated Religious.

And at Last:
In honor of Mother, Father, Sister and Brother –
who nurtured, challenged and inspired Evan in their humble
Phamily of five.
-

And in eternal gratitude to the Blessed Virgin Mary – Queen of Heaven and
Earth, Her Son – Our Lord Jesus Christ, His Father and ours – the Almighty,
and Their Love – the Holy Spirit.
-

And with profound thanks to you – beloved reader –
for sharing your time with this tale.

AFTERWORD
(Spoiler Alert!)

= = =

The subject of demon redeeming, a redeemer of demons, demon redemption, etc. is a theological impossibility. The sins of man are forgivable in that man acts largely in ignorance ["Father, forgive them; for they know not what they do." -LUKE 23:34], whereas the sin of the fallen angels was acted not in ignorance but in unhindered intellect, will, full knowledge, freedom, and deliberation. Hence this novel is a work of theological fiction, wrought from wandering in God – wandering love, wandering His limitless grace and mercy, His boundless truth, beauty, and goodness.

Yet, also worth wandering in are the words of SAINT GABRIEL THE ARCHANGEL:
"For with God nothing will be impossible."
-LUKE 1:37

Meet Her Maker:

= = =

EVAN PHAM listens to his heartbeat and translates it. The silence of his monk cell in rural Michigan allows him to interpret his soul's ache for art that not merely attracts the eye, but woos eyes to fall in love with sight, courts ears to marriage with music, arouses the senses to consummation with creation.

But sometimes Evan just plain loves filling that silence with good music and movies. Let him know your favorites and it just might help him dream his next novel into flesh.

You can tell Evan at:
FaceBook.com/LittleMissLucifer
or at: LittleMissLucifer.com

This is Evan's first novel.

Meet Her Publisher:

= = =

BANNED BOOKS PRESS is firmly committed to publishing quality crafted works that expose the anonymous power and emphasize the reality of certain societies, nations and areas of the world where being Christian and proclaiming the Gospel are restricted, illegal and considered offensive. Penalties for Christians in these areas include fines, unjust discrimination, imprisonment, torture and even death.

HELP HER:
[ALL GIRLS ALLOWED]

= = =

Each year, millions of Chinese girls are culled before or after their birth because of the Chinese Communist Party's draconian One-Child Policy, and because of unjust cultural discrimination. Today, at least 37 million women and girls are missing in China – and those who survive the continued culling are considered illegal children, and their mothers and fathers are illegal parents.

LITTLE MISS LUCIFER is a story that stares down this horrific reality, that seeks to battle this and other evils. When Evan finished authoring and began editing the story, he remembered stumbling upon a way to help. He decided to act.

ALL GIRLS ALLOWED is a non-profit and non-government organization that helps China's millions of unloved girls and women live and thrive in an unloving and unjust time.

To help, 15% of all profits from LITTLE MISS LUCIFER sales will be donated straight to ALL GIRLS ALLOWED.

But of course that is not enough. Please consider visiting the AGA website to learn more about this important mission, and please consider supporting the cause according to your will and ability.

[ALLGIRLSALLOWED.ORG]

聖 彌 額 爾 總 領 天 使

在戰爭的日子裡保衛我們，免我們
陷入魔鬼邪惡的陰謀，和奸詐的陷
阱中。我們謙卑地祈求，但願上主
譴責牠。上天萬軍的統帥，求你因
上主的威能，把淮迴人間，引誘人
靈，使其喪亡的撒殫及其他邪靈，
抛下地獄裡去。
亞們。

SAINT MICHAEL THE ARCHANGEL

defend us in battle. Be our safeguard against
the wickedness and the snares of the devil.
May God rebuke him, we humbly pray – and
do thou, oh Prince of the Heavenly Host, by
the divine power of God, cast into Hell, Satan
and all the evil spirits, who prowl about the
world seeking the ruin of souls.
Amen.

Sancte Míchaël Archángele

deFénde nos in prœlio;
contra nequítiam et insídias
diáboli esto præsídium.
ímperet illi deus.
súpplices deprecámur.
tuque. princeps milítiæ cæléstis.
sátanam aliósque spíritus malígnos.
qui ad perditiónem animárum
pervagántur in mundo.
divína virtúte. in inférnum detrúde.
amen.

Lord, have mercy on us...
Christ, have mercy on us...
Lord, have mercy on us...

Christ, hear us...
Christ, graciously hear us...

God the Father of Heaven...
God the Son, Redeemer of the world...
God the Holy Ghost...
Holy Trinity, One God...

Holy Mary...
Holy Mother of God...
Holy Virgin of virgins...

Saint Michael...
Saint Gabriel...
Saint Raphael...
All ye holy Angels and Archangels...
All ye holy orders of blessed Spirits...

Saint John the Baptist...
Saint Joseph...
All ye holy Patriarchs and Prophets...

Saint Peter...
Saint Paul...
Saint Andrew...
Saint James...
Saint John...
Saint Thomas...
Saint James...
Saint Philip...
Saint Bartholomew...
Saint Matthew...
Saint Simon...
Saint Thaddeus...
Saint Matthias...
Saint Barnabas...
Saint Luke...
Saint Mark...
All ye holy Apostles and Evangelists...
All ye holy Disciples of the Lord...

All ye holy Innocents...
Saint Stephen...
Saint Lawrence...
Saint Vincent...
Saints Fabian and Sebastian...
Saints John and Paul...
Saints Cosmas and Damian...
Saints Gervase and Protase...
All ye holy Martyrs...

Saint Sylvester...
Saint Gregory...
Saint Ambrose...
Saint Augustine...
Saint Jerome...
Saint Martin...
Saint Nicholas...
All ye holy Bishops and Confessors...
All ye holy Doctors...

Saint Anthony...
Saint Benedict...
Saint Bernard...
Saint Dominic...
Saint Francis...
All ye holy Priests and Levites...
All ye holy Monks and Hermits...

Saint Anne...
Saint Philomena...
Saint Teresa...
Saint Rosa...
Saint Monica...
Saint Elizabeth...
Saint Mary Magdalen...
Saint Agatha...
Saint Lucy...
Saint Agnes...
Saint Cecilia...
Saint Catherine...
Saint Barbara...
Saint Anastasia...
All ye holy Virgins and Widows...

All ye holy Saints of God...

KÝRIE, ELÉISON
CHRISTE, ELÉISON
KÝRIE, ELÉISON

(This part is actually
in **Greek**, not Latin!)

MISERÉRE EA/EO/NOBIS: Have mercy on her/him/us
ORÁ(TE) PRO EA/EO/NOBIS: Pray for her/him/us
[Please note: the Litany of the Saints presented here and in the novel is far from complete.]

母后萬福，仁慈的母親，我們的生命，我們的甘飴，我們的希望。厄娃子孫，在此塵世，向您哀呼。在這涕泣之谷，向您歎息哭求。我們的主保，求您回顧憐視我們。一但流亡期滿，使我們得見您的聖子，萬民稱頌的耶穌。童貞瑪利亞，您是寬仁的、慈悲的、甘飴的。天主聖母，請為我們祈求，使我們堪受基督的恩許。阿們。